Anybody But Anne

By Carolyn Wells

Originally published in 1914

Anybody But Anne

© 2011 Resurrected Press
www.ResurrectedPress.com

Published by Resurrected Press

This classic book was handcrafted by Resurrected Press. Resurrected Press is dedicated to bringing high quality classic books back to the readers who enjoy them. These are not scanned versions of the originals, but, rather, quality checked and edited books meant to be enjoyed!

Please visit ResurrectedPress.com to view our entire catalogue!

ISBN 13: 978-1-937022-34-1

Printed in the United States of America

Other Resurrected Press Mysteries

FOREWORD

Carolyn Wells was well known for her many mysteries in which some architectural device such as a secret panel or passage plays a role. Locked room mysteries, in which a murder has been committed in a chamber sealed from the inside, were much in vogue in the period in which Wells wrote, and she was always happy to appeal to the public's taste. *Anybody but Anne* features one of the more clever of her puzzles.

Anybody but Anne also features that most unusual of detectives, Fleming Stone. Unlike many of the famous detectives of the period, Stone is neither a wealthy dilettante nor an eccentric genius, but instead has taken up detection as a serious profession. He is described as a distinguished middle aged man of medium height, a man of education and refinement, but is without the quirks or unusual interests that seem to be so common to the fictional detectives of the period.

In one respect he is markedly different than the typical detective. He rarely makes an appearance until the final few chapters of the mystery, though various of the characters may make reference to him throughout the book as they debate whether to call in the great detective. When he final does make his appearance, he makes a brief inspection of the scene of the crime, examines a few clues, asks a few seemingly random questions of various servants and witnesses and then in the final chapter announces his conclusions. There is rarely a weighing of the evidence or eliminating of suspects, instead, he has the ability to notice the one crucial piece of information that has eluded all other sleuths either official or amateur.

In *Anybody but Anne*, Stone does make a brief appearance in the early part of the book where he is called upon to give a demonstration of his powers of observation with a parlor trick. From a woman's fan, he deduces a host of particulars about the owner's life. He then vanishes from the intervening chapters until he reappears at the end to solve the mystery.

Fleming Stone would appear in dozens of mysteries by Carolyn Wells, proving to be the most popular of her detectives.

The early mysteries of Carolyn Wells, in addition to being entertaining, give the reader a glimpse into American society pre-World War I, a world where there were still great mansions and large family fortunes, but a world that was even then vanishing.

It is with great pleasure that Resurrected Press offers its readers this new edition of *Anybody but Anne*.

About the Author

Carolyn Wells, June 18, 1862 March 26, 1942 was an American writer and poet. She was best known for her books of poetry and humor until around 1910 she read one of Anna Katherine Green's mysteries and took up the genre. Many of her mysteries featured the detective Fleming Stone. She was married to Hadwin Houghton, heir to the Houghton-Mifflin publishing company. She was a collector of poetry by other authors, and, upon her death, she bequeathed her collection of the works of Walt Witman to the Library of Congress.

Greg Fowlkes
Editor-In-Chief
Resurrected Press
www.ResurrectedPress.com

TABLE OF CONTENTS

CHAPTER 1: BUTTONWOOD TERRACE

THE letter I had just read was signed Anne Mansfield Van Wyck,—and the first two names gave my memory such a fillip, that I sat for a long time, motionless, while my thoughts raced back ten years, and reached their goal in a little suburban town. The picture which memory so obligingly showed me, in definite detail, was that of two young people saying good-by, somewhat effusively. One of these was an immature version of my present self, and the other was a pigtailed school-girl, who now signed herself, Anne Mansfield Van Wyck. At the time of that dramatic parting, she had been Anne Mansfield, and I, Raymond Sturgis, was leaving her to go to college.

Our farewell promises, though made in all good faith, were never fulfilled; and the barrier of circumstances that time raised between us, had kept us from sight of each other for ten years.

I assumed, when I thought of it at all, that Anne had forgotten me; and though I had not forgotten her, I remembered her only casually, and at long intervals.

I had heard of her marriage to David Van Wyck without poignant regret, but with a feeling of resentment that she should throw herself away on a man so old and eccentric, though a well-known capitalist.

And, now, all unexpectedly, I had received an invitation to one of her house parties. It expressed, pleasantly enough, a desire to renew our old-time acquaintance, and asked me to come on Friday for the week-end.

The stationery was correct and rather elegant; the handwriting fashionable and sophisticated,—not at all like the sprawling school-girl hand of ten years ago.

My curiosity was roused to know what Anne would be like as Mrs. Van Wyck, and I accepted the invitation with a pleased sense of regaining an old friend.

As my train swayed swiftly through New England, toward the village of Crescent Falls, where the Van Wycks had their summer residence, I tried to picture to myself the pretty little Anne Mansfield that I had known, as the chatelaine of a great estate, with an elderly husband and two grown-up step-children.

The picture was so incongruous that I gave it up, and awaited first impressions with unbiased opinions.And I may well have done so, for, though I knew of his wealth, I knew nothing of the taste and judgment that had led David Van Wyck to select for his summer home a most beautiful country estate, whose century-old mansion was surrounded by equally old buttonwood trees, a species rapidly growing extinct in New England.

The motor car which brought me from the station swung into the broad avenue that led to the house, and I marvelled that such a home could have been found in America. For it was like an English park; the green lawns rolling off in velvety sweeps toward distances of woodland, which betokened flowery dells and picturesque ravines.

No one had met me at the railroad station, save the chauffeur and footman, so I assumed that the Van Wyck household was conducted on formal lines. I held my mind open for informing impressions, and suddenly, rounding a curve, we came within sight of the house.

I knew the Van Wyck home was called Buttonwood Terrace, but when I saw it I felt a whimsical impulse to call it All Gaul—for it was so definitely divided into three parts. The enormous rectangle that had originally formed the main dwelling had later received the addition of two also rectangular wings. But these were not attached in the usual fashion; they were jauntily caught by their corners to the two rear corners of the main house. These lapping walls impinged but a few feet, or just enough for communicating doors. Thus, the wings, with the back or southern side of the house, formed three sides of a delightful terrace, from which marble steps and grassy paths led to formal gardens beyond, where one could wander among fountains, statues, and rare and beautiful plants.

The West wing held the many kitchens and other servants' quarters, and the East wing,—I judged from its long, almost church-like windows,—was a great hall of some sort.

For some reason, the car circled the house before pausing at the front entrance, and, enthralled by the beauty and wonder of the place, I was ready to forgive Anne Mansfield her much-criticized marriage. The door was opened to me by an obsequious personage in livery, and I was at once shown to my room. This was on the second floor, at the front of the house, and on the East side. It was a marvel of good taste and comfortable, even luxurious appointments, but I scarcely noticed it, as I caught sight of the view from my windows.

The Berkshire hills rolled above and beyond one another, in what seemed a very riot of mountainous glee. The spring green had appeared early, and the tender verdure of the young leaves contrasted with the deep greens and purples of the mountain forests. It was nearly sunset, and a red gold glow added a theatrical effect to the glorious landscape. I leaned out of my East window, and glanced toward the back of the house. I saw again that great East wing, so peculiarly attached to the corner of the main dwelling, and concluded it had been built later. It had almost the appearance of a chapel, for the long windows were of stained glass, with arched tops and ornate casings. The fact that these windows reached from the roof nearly to the ground, proved the wing apartment to be a lofty one, fully the height of two ordinary stories. So interested in the matter was I, that I asked the man who was unpacking my things, if the East wing might be a chapel.

"No, sir," he answered; "it's Mr. Van Wyck's study."

He volunteered the further information that tea was now being served there, and that I was to go down as soon as I was ready.

Shortly after, I followed my guide through the halls and rooms of the enormous house. Drawingrooms and reception rooms were furnished with quiet elegance; and the heavy hangings, though of brocades and tapestries, were never obtrusive in coloring or design.

Through the halls we went, until we reached the doorway that formed the sole connection between the main house and the East wing. Here, after a murmured announcement of my name, the servant left me, and I found myself in the study of David Van Wyck.

I think I have never seen a more impressive room than this study at Buttonwood Terrace. Its domed ceiling of leaded glass was perhaps thirty feet high, but so large was the room and so graceful its lines that the architecture gave the effect of perfect proportion.

The walls were panelled between the stainedglass windows, and at the West end of the room was a small balcony, like a musicians' gallery, reached by a spiral staircase. At the same end of the room, under the balcony and opening on the terrace, were large double doors; and there was no other entrance save the single door that connected with the main house through the lapped corners.

There were perhaps a dozen people present, and though, of course, I recognized my hostess, I went to greet her with a face that, I am sure, showed an expression of incredulity.

Anne Van Wyck laughed outright.

"It's really I," she said; "you seem unable to believe it—"

But even before I could reply she turned to welcome another newcomer, and I stood alone, a moment, waiting for her to turn back to me.

The scene was a picturesque one. The contrast of the modern garbed society people, their light laughter and gay chatter, with the dignity and grandeur of the old room and its antique furnishings, made an interesting picture. Everywhere the eye rested on carvings and tapestries worthy of a baronial hall, and yet the gay occupation of afternoon tea seemed not amiss in this setting. It was late in May, and though the great doors stood open to the terrace, the blaze of an open fire was not ungrateful. My hostess did not herself preside at the teatable, but left that to her step-daughter Barbara, while she graciously dispensed charming smiles of greeting or farewell to the guests who came or went.

After a few moments came a lull in her duties and with a fascinating smile she invited me to sit beside her and talk over old times.

"Remembering our schoolmate days, may I call you Anne?" I asked, taking my place by her on a divan.

"I suppose I really oughtn't to allow it, but it is pleasant to feel you are an old friend," she smiled.

"It is—though a bit hard to realize that the little school-girl I used to know is now mistress of all this grandeur."

"It is a fine old place, isn't it?" she returned, evading the personal equation. "And, perhaps because of its picturesque possibilities, I pride myself on my house-parties. I adore having guests, and I invite them with an eye to their fitting into this environment."

"Thank you for the implied compliment," I murmured, but I brought back my gaze from my surroundings, to look more attentively at Anne's face.

It seemed to me I had caught a plaintive note in her voice, and I looked for a corresponding expression in her eyes. But she dropped her long lashes, after a swift glance that was a little roguish, a little wistful, and entirely fascinating. Suddenly I wondered if she were happy. My vague impression of her husband was that he was tyrannical and possibly cruel; I felt intuitively that

Anne's lightheartedness was assumed, and covered a disappointed life.

But meantime she was chatting on, gaily. "Yes," she declared; "I select my house-parties with the utmost care. I have an exactly proper admixture of married people and unmarried, of serious-minded and frivolous, of geniuses and feather-heads."

"In which class am I?" I asked, more for the sake of making her look at me than for a desire for information.

"It's so long since we last met, that I shall have to study you a bit before I can classify you. But please be as frivolous as you can, for I want you to offset a very serious guest."

"I know," I said, following Anne's glance across the room; "the long girl in pale green. I shall have to be a veritable buffoon to average up with that serious-minded siren! She looks like a Study of a Wailing Soul."

"Yes—isn't she Burne-Jonesey? That's Beth Fordyce, and she's the dearest thing in the world, but she has a sort of aesthetic pose, and goes in a little for the occult and such ridiculous things. But you'll like her, for she's a dear when she forgets her fad."

"Does she ever forget it?"

"Yes; when she's thinking of clothes. Indeed, sometimes I think she prefers clothes to soul fulness, — but she's terribly devoted to both."

"She certainly makes a success of her raiment," I observed, looking at the long, sweeping lines of Miss Fordyce's misty, green draperies.

I suppose it was only a touch of the Eternal Feminine, but Anne seemed to resent my compliment to the green gown, and quickly turned the subject.

"The frizzy blonde lady next her is Mrs. Stelton," she went on; "she's a young widow who's terribly in love with Morland, my step-son. To tell the truth, I invited her because I want him to find out that he really doesn't care for her, after all. Then Barbara, at the tea-table is my step-daughter; she's exactly like her father, and when I married him, Barbara was determined not to like me. But I am determined she shall; and of course I shall win out—though I haven't made any startling success as yet."

"So much for the women," I said. "Now tell me of your men."

"Well, you know my husband. He's distinguished-looking, isn't he? And though he's nearly sixty, that little alert air of his makes him seem younger. Morland looks like him, but they are not at all alike otherwise. Morland is handsome but he is puffy-minded, and any woman can lead him by a string. For the moment, he thinks Mrs. Stelton is his ideal, but I intend that Beth Fordyce shall dethrone her. That tall man talking to Beth now is Connie Archer. He's a dear thing, but a little difficult. Mr. Van Wyck doesn't like him; but, then, my husband likes so few people."

"Do you like Mr. Archer?" I asked, looking directly at her.

She flashed me a glance of surprise, and then answered coolly, "I like him, but not as much as he likes me."

"Anne Mansfield Van Wyck," I said, looking at her sternly, "don't tell me you've developed into a coquette!"

"Developed!" she repeated, with a gay little laugh; "I was always a coquette. I used to flirt with you, 'way back in High School Days."

"That you did!" I agreed. "You purposely kept Jim Lucas and me in a fever of jealousy toward one another!"

"Of course I did. You were both so susceptible. If I let one of you carry my schoolbooks, the other promptly went off in a sulk." Anne laughed merrily at the recollection, and I gazed at her, thinking how beautiful she had grown, and wondering why she had married Van Wyck.

"And do you remember," I went on, a little diffidently, "the last time we met?"

"'Deed I do!" she replied, without a trace of embarrassment. "You were going off to college, and you kissed my hand as we parted. That was a very graceful

act,—for a school-boy,—and I've never forgotten how well
you did it."

"Yes," said I, lightly, "one must be a born cavalier to
get away with a hand-kiss successfully. When I get a real
good chance I'm going to see if your right hand has lost its
cunning."

"Nonsense!" she returned laughingly. "I'm not allowed
to permit anything of that sort. I'm a perfect Griselda of a
wife and my husband rules me with a rod of iron."

"Indeed I do," said Van Wyck himself, as he came
toward us, and, really, Anne's speech had been made at
him rather than to me.

"And so you knew my wife as a child?" he asked, after
Anne had conventionally introduced us.

"As a girl," I corrected him. "We were acquainted
during our High School days, when I was an awkward
cub, and she was ' standing with reluctant feet.'"

"H'm; and was she then, as now, a self-willed;
insistent creature, determined to have her own way in
everything?"

My blood boiled at his tone, even more than at his
words. But I felt sure it was better to keep to the light
key, so I said: "Yes, indeed; like all other women. And
even as boys, we men are only too glad to give the Blessed
Sex their own way."

Anne flashed me a glance that distinctly betokened
approval. I felt she had wondered how I would meet her
husband's ill-chosen speech, and I felt an elation at
having passed through the ordeal successfully in her
eyes.

David Van Wyck glowered at me. As Anne had said,
he was distinguished-looking, but his drawn brows, and
straight, thin lips, showed habitual surliness. His thick,
tossing hair was almost white, and his acutely black eyes
gleamed from beneath heavy gray eyebrows. He was tall
and well-proportioned, with an alert air that made him
seem less than the sixty years his wife had ascribed to
him.

He was handsome; his manners, though superficial, were correct; and yet he roused in me a spirit of antagonism such as no stranger ever had done before. After a few moments more conversation, he said, quite abruptly, "I will take your place beside my wife, and do you go and make yourself charming to the other ladies."

CHAPTER 2: THE VAN WYCK HOUSEHOLD

"PRESENTLY," I returned equably; "but first let me congratulate you on the find of this delightful old place. This room itself is a marvel. It might have been brought over from some English castle."

David Van Wyck looked around appreciatively. "It is a fine room," he agreed. "It was built later than the main house, and was originally intended, I imagine, for a ballroom. It has a specially fine floor, and that musicians' gallery at the end seems to indicate festivities on a big scale. To be sure, the whole scheme of decoration is too massive and over-ornate for these days, but it is all in harmony, and the gorgeousness of coloring has been toned down by time."

This was true. The lofty walls were topped by a wide and heavy cornice, with an enormous cartouche in each corner, massive enough for a cathedral. But the coloring was dimmed by the years, and the gilding was tarnished to a soft bronze. Most of the furniture consisted of choice old pieces collected by Van Wyck for this especial use, and it was plain to be seen that he took great pride in these, and in his rare and valuable pictures and curios.

"It is my room," he was saying, as he smiled benignly on his wife, "but I let Anne have her fal-lal teas here, because she thinks it's picturesque. But except at the tea-hour, this is my exclusive domain."

"You call it your study?" I inquired casually.

"I call it my study, yes; although I'm not a studious man, by any means. It is really my office, I suppose; but such a name would never fit this eighteenth-century atmosphere. I have my desk here, and my secretaries and lawyers come when I call them, and I have even profaned the place with a telephone, so that I'm always in touch

with what the poets call the busy mart. Moreover, I
confess I'm subject to short-lived fads and fancies, and
this goodsized room gives me space to indulge my interest
of the moment."

"He is, indeed," said Anne, laughing. "Last summer he
was a naturalist, and this room was full of stuffed birds
and dried beetles and all sorts of awful things. But that's
all over now, and this year —what are you this year,
David?"

Van Wyck's face hardened. A steely look came into
his eyes, and his square jaw set itself more firmly, as he
replied, in a dry, curt tone, "I'm a philanthropist."

The word seemed simple enough, and yet Anne's face
also became suddenly serious, and. unless I was
mistaken, a flash of anger shot from her dark eyes to her
husband's grim face. But just then Archer and Miss
Fordyce joined us, and Anne's smiles returned instantly.

"What mood, Beth?" she cried gaily. "You see, Honey,
I've been telling Mr. Sturgis that you're aesthetic and
lanky-minded and all the rest of it, and you must live up
to your reputation."

"If I can," murmured Miss Fordyce, rolling a pair of
soulful blue eyes at me; "but I'm only a beginner—a
disciple of the wonderful mysticism of the—"

"There, there, Beth, cut it short," broke in Archer. "We
know! The mysticism of the theosophical value of the
occult as applied to the hyperasstheticism of the soul by
whichever Great High Muck-a-Muck you've been reading
last."

The others laughed, but Miss Fordyce gave the
speaker a reproachful glance, which, however, utterly
failed to wither him.

"You'd be a real nice girl, Beth," he went on, "if you'd
chuck mysticism and go in for athletics."

"You don't understand, Mr. Archer," began Miss
Fordyce, in her soft, melodious voice; but Archer
interrupted her:

"Now, don't come the misunderstood racket on me! I won't stand for it. Practise your wiles on Mr. Sturgis. Take him over there, and show him Mr. Van Wyck's Buddha, and tell him what you know about Buddhaing as a fine art."

I walked away with the pale-haired Miss Fordyce, but instead of talking about Buddha, we naturally fell into conversation about our fellow-guests.

"I can well understand," I said slowly, "that the occult would scarcely appeal to such a practical specimen of manhood as Archer. Who is he and what is he?"

"To begin with, he's a supreme egotist."

"Oh, I don't mean his character; but what does he do?"

"I don't know, exactly. I believe he's a mining engineer or something. But he's terribly in love with Anne, and he's clever enough not to let Mr. Van Wyck know it."

"But Anne knows it?"

"Of course, yes; and she doesn't care two cents for him. But she's a born coquette, and she leads him on, for nothing but an idle amusement. I don't think a woman ought to do that."

"Doubtless you are right, Miss Fordyce; but is it your experience that women always do what they ought to do?"

"Very rarely," returned Miss Fordyce, laughing, and I began to realize that when the girl dropped her silly pose, she was really charming. "And especially Anne," she went on. "She's one of my dearest friends, but that doesn't blind me to her faults."

"And is it a fault to be attractive?"

"To be as attractive as Anne Van Wyck is a crime." Miss Fordyce smiled as she spoke, but there was a ring of earnestness in her tone. "She is a siren, and her charm is of the sort that bowls men over before they know what they're about."

"I'm glad you warned me," I returned; "I'll be on my guard against her fatal glances."

"You've known her a long time, haven't you?"

"Oh, no; I knew her ten years ago, as a schoolgirl, but she doesn't seem to be the same Anne now."

"She's a dear!" exclaimed Miss Fordyce, warmheartedly, "and I have done wrong in even seeming to censure her. But she does lead men a dance."

"Isn't she afraid of her husband?"

"Anne is afraid of nobody on earth,—well, with one exception,—but the exception is not her husband."

"Who is it then? You?"

"Oh, goodness, no! Why should she be afraid of me? But she is afraid of Mrs. Carstairs, the housekeeper."

"The housekeeper! How curious. Why is it?"

"I don't know. But Mrs. Carstairs is really a most peculiar person. She was housekeeper for Mr. Van Wyck before Anne married him. Her son is Mr. Van Wyck's valet. Well, Anne would be glad to send them both packing, mother and son, but her husband won't let her."

"Why not?"

"Oh, he is accustomed to their ways,—and they are both remarkably capable."

"But why is Anne afraid of them?"

"I don't think she's afraid of Carstairs. But the mother is so queer. Anne says she has the evil eye."

"Aren't you and Anne imagining these things? Isn't it one of your 'occult' notions?"

"Wait till you see Mrs. Carstairs. You'll realize at once she's queer."

"I thought a housekeeper was always a portly, placid, middle-aged woman, in a black silk dress."

Beth Fordyce laughed, "You couldn't guess farther from the mark! Mrs. Carstairs is not middleaged. Indeed, she seems extremely young to be the mother of the valet. He must be over twenty. Then she is very good looking, with a dark, subtle sort of beauty. She's small, and slender, and she glides about so softly, she seems to appear from nowhere. Why, there she is now!"

I looked across the room and saw Mrs. Carstairs speaking to Anne. She wore black silk, it is true; but of modish cut and long, graceful lines. Indeed, she seemed to have more of an air of distinction than any of the other women present, excepting Anne. She had no touch of apology or obsequiousness in her manner, and stood quietly talking, until she had finished her errand, and then moved away, and left the room without embarrassment. Her selfpoise was marvellous, and I felt a flash of regret that such a woman should have to pursue what was after all, a menial occupation.

"She looks interesting," I remarked to Miss Fordyce.

"She is!" was the emphatic reply. "Of course, it's an open secret that she hoped to marry Mr. Van Wyck. She was housekeeper here when he was a widower. Then, when he married Anne, he insisted that Mrs. Carstairs should stay on, to relieve Anne of all housekeeping boredom."

"And Anne doesn't want her?"

"Not a bit; but she can't persuade Mr. Van Wyck to discharge her. The valet is most satisfactory, I believe, and the mother and son refuse to be separated. So, they're both here. But Anne is afraid of her."

"How absurd!"

"I don't know. Mrs. Carstairs hates Anne, and though she is never openly disrespectful, she finds hundreds of little ways to annoy her."

"And Anne's step-children? How does she get along with them?"

"Oh, right enough. Morland adores her, and though Barbara was offish at first, she is coming round. Anne has shown great tact in managing Barbara, and I think they'll get to be chums."

I hadn't yet had opportunity to converse with Barbara Van Wyck, and under pretense of a quest of fresh tea, I led Miss Fordyce toward the tea-table. Miss Van Wyck was cordial, but not effusive, and struck me as being what is sometimes called "strong-minded."

She was a striking-looking girl, with a pale face and large dark eyes; but she had no such charm as Anne, nor had she the gentle softness of Beth Fordyce. She managed the tea-things with a graceful air of being accustomed to it, and included us at once in a conversation she was carrying on with some other callers.

It seemed the Van Wyck tea hour was something of an institution; and neighbors and village people were always in greater or less attendance.

The discussion was concerning a new public library in the town, and as it was of slight interest to me, I permitted my attention to wander about the room, and began to plan some way by which I could unobtrusively make my way back to my hostess. But just then a motor-car arrived, and a group of callers came in through the great portals of the study. The general confusion of introductions and greetings followed, and when it was over I somehow found myself standing beside Mrs. Stelton, the pretty young widow from whose toils Anne hoped to rescue Morland Van Wyck.

She was attractive in her way, but commonplace compared to Beth Fordyce or Anne. She chatted pleasantly, but her conversation was of the sort that makes a man's mind wander.

"Are you here for the week end, Mr. Sturgis?" she rattled on; "you'll have a heavenly time! It's the dearest place to visit. And they are all such lovely people. The beautiful Mrs. Van Wyck is a perfect hostess,—and Mr. Van Wyck is an old dear, —though a bit of a curmudgeon now and then."

"You're speaking of Mr. Morland Van Wyck?" I teased.

"You naughty man! Of course not. I mean our host. Morly isn't in the least curmudgeonish!"

She tapped my arm with her lorgnon in a playful manner. "As if any one could be,—to you," I returned, knowing her type.

"Nice gentleman!" she babbled on. "I admit I like a compliment now and then. I'm glad you're here. We're such a pleasant house-party."

"Who is that striking-looking man standing by the window?" I asked. "We were introduced as he came in, but I didn't catch his name."

"Stone," she replied, "Fleming Stone. They say he is a detective."

"Stone!" I exclaimed. "Is it really? Detective! I should think he was! Why, he's probably the greatest real detective who ever lived! What is he doing here?"

"His home is in Crescent Falls," Mrs. Stelton informed me; "that is, his mother has recently come here to live in the village, and he, naturally, visits her. He is staying with her now."

"Is he a friend of Van Wyck's?"

"No, he has never been here before. He came with Mr. and Mrs. Davidson, Crescent Falls Village people, and I think he came principally to see the house. This room, you know, is famous."

"Not as famous as he is," I said, gazing at the man I so much admired, but had never before seen. Fleming Stone was a man who would have compelled notice anywhere, and yet his appearance was entirely quiet and unostentatious. He was slightly above average height, of a strong, well set up figure and a forceful expression of face. His hair was slightly gray at the temples, and his dark, deep-set eyes gave a strangely blended effect of unerring vision and kindly judgment. His manner was marked by a gentle courtesy, and his personal magnetism was apparent in every tone and gesture.

I longed to get away from the uninteresting widow and talk or at least listen to Mr. Stone. As this was not possible, I suggested that we both stroll across the room and join the group that surrounded him. Though apparently not over-anxious, Mrs. Stelton agreed to this, and we became a part of the small circle that had formed around the great detective.

Great detective I knew him to be, for his fame was world-wide, and yet as he stood there drinking his tea with a careless grace, he gave only the impression of a cultured society man, ready to lend himself to the polite idle chatter of the moment. He was looking at Anne Van Wyck, and, though not staring, not even gazing intently, I could see that his interest centred in her.

But this was not at all astonishing. I think few men were ever in Anne Van Wyck's presence without centring their interest upon her.

Her slender figure was exquisitely proportioned, and her small head, with its masses of soft dark hair, was set upon her shoulders with a marvellous grace. Her deep gray eyes, with long, curling, dark lashes, were full of fascination, and her small, pale face was capable of expressing such receptiveness and such responsiveness that one's eyes were drawn to it irresistibly. Anne's face was mysterious—purposely so, maybe, for she was intensely clever; but mysterious with the weird fascination of the Sphinx. And as Fleming Stone's own deep eyes met those of Anne Van Wyck, in a glance that caught and held, it seemed as if two similar natures experienced a mutual recognition.

I may have been over-fanciful, but I looked upon Fleming Stone as almost superhuman; and though, before my arrival at Buttonwood Terrace, I had felt no special personal interest in Mrs. David Van Wyck, I was now conscious of a dawning realization that the Anne Mansfield I used to know had grown to a wonderful woman.

It was part of Anne's beautiful tact, that she made no reference to Fleming Stone's profession or to his celebrity.

She smiled graciously and opened the conversation with a bit of banter.

"It is a great pleasure to welcome you under our roof-tree, Mr. Stone," she was saying, "but it is also a surprise. For, I am told, you are a confirmed woman-hater."

"Aren't 'woman-haters' always confirmed, Mrs. Van Wyck?" he parried; "I never heard of one that wasn't."

"Nor I," said Anne, laughing at the quip; "but you evade my question. Do you hate all women?"

"No," said Stone; "I do not. But if I did, I should say I did not,—out of common politeness."

"How baffling!" cried Anne. "Now I can form no idea of your attitude toward our sex."

"Oh, I've no reason to conceal that," said Stone, lightly. "It is merely the attitude of civilized man toward civilized woman. Taken collectively, women are delightful. But any one of them alone, nearly scares me out of my wits."

"I'd like to try it!" said Anne, with a daring sweep of her long lashes, as she half closed her eyes, and looked at him.

"You wouldn't have to try. I admit I'm afraid of you already. I'm afraid of any woman. One never knows what they mean by what they say."

"They rarely know that, themselves," Anne flung back at him; and Condon Archer, who stood near, added, "Or if they do, they know wrong."

"These are cryptic utterances," I put in, laughingly. "Are you good people sure you know what you're talking about?"

"We're sure we don't!" said Anne, gaily, "and that's just as good. But if we're really achieving cryptic remarks, we'll refer them to Beth. She knows all about crypticism,—or whatever you call it,—and mysticism, and occultism--"

"Oh, good gracious, Anne, don't!" cried Miss Fordyce. "I don't mind people who understand, talking about those things; but you are not only ignorant but intolerant of them."

"Nonsense, girlie," said Anne, smiling at Miss Fordyce, "I love you, and so I love all those crazy notions of yours."

"I'm sure Mr. Stone understands," Beth Fordyce went on, looking at him with earnest eyes.

It may have been my imagination, but it seemed to me that Fleming Stone had to wrench his attention away from Anne by force, and compel himself to reply to Miss Fordyce's remark.

CHAPTER 3: ALL ABOUT A FAN

"You are sure I understand what, Miss Fordyce?" he asked; "I assure you my understanding is not limitless."

"Oh, understand clairvoyance, and all that sort of thing. You must, you know, with all your wonderful detective ability. Please tell us all about yourself, won't you? I never saw a real detective before, and they're awfully different from what I imagined! I thought they were more—more "

"Unwashed," put in Archer bluntly. "I am not myself acquainted with many of them, but those I have met are not in Mr. Stone's class socially, by any means."

"They're not in his class professionally, either," I declared, anxious to have Fleming Stone aware of my appreciation of his genius. "Mr. Stone is in a class by himself. His work is art, that's what it is."

"Thank you," said Fleming Stone, but in the smile he gave me there was a slight tinge of that boredness that masters always feel at compliments from tyros. "My art, as you call it, is my life," he went on, simply. "I do not study it, I simply practise it as it comes along. And, after all, any success I may have had is merely the rational outcome of logical observation."

"Oh, don't depreciate yourself, Mr. Stone," said Mrs. Stelton, shaking a silly finger at him. "You know you are the greatest detective ever— Mr. Sturgis told me so. And now you must, you simply must, tell us just how you do it, and give us an example. Here, take my fan, and deduce my whole mental calibre from it!"

Although Fleming Stone looked at the speaker pleasantly, I was convinced that he felt, as I did, that it would be perfectly easy to deduce the lady's mental calibre without the assistance of her lace fan.

"Yes, do! What fun!" exclaimed Morland Van Wyck, who was standing at the elbow of the fair widow who had enslaved him.

Before Fleming Stone could reply, Anne spoke. "That wouldn't be a fair test," she said, flashing a smile at Stone; and then her eyes curiously deepened with earnestness as she went on: "But I do wish, Mr. Stone, that you would do something like that for us. I have heard that you can tell all about any one, just from seeing some article that they have used."

"That is not a difficult thing to do, Mrs. Van Wyck," said Stone. "You yourself could probably gather a great deal of information from any personal belonging of a stranger."

"Oh, yes," returned Anne gaily; "if I saw a thimble, I might deduce a sewing-woman; or a pipe, a man who smoked. But I don't mean that—I mean the sort of thing you do. Please give us an example." I fairly cringed at the thought of Fleming Stone being stood up to do parlor tricks, like a society circus; and so incensed was I that the line, "Butchered to make a Roman holiday," vaguely passed through my mind. But as I saw Anne's vivid, glowing face and her entreating eyes, I felt sure that no man on earth could deny her anything.

Stone appeared to take it casually. "Certainly, Mrs. Van Wyck," he said, "if it will please you. I have never done such a thing, except in the interests of my work, but if you will give me a personal belonging of some one unknown to me, I will repeat to you whatever it may tell me concerning its owner."

Though Beth Fordyce had said nothing during this latter conversation, I think she had never once moved her eyes from Stone's face. Her large and light blue eyes looked at him with an absorbed gaze, and she spoke, tranquilly, but with a positive air.

"I will provide the article," she said. "I have with me just the very thing. Excuse me, I will get it."

She glided away—for no other verb of motion expresses her peculiar walk—and disappeared through the door that led into the main part of the house.

"How lovely!" cried Mrs. Stelton, clasping her hands in delight. "And then, Mr. Stone, will you tell us how you catch robbers by their foot-prints?"

"Alas, madam," said Stone, "robbers are rarely considerate enough to leave their foot-prints for my benefit. I know they have the reputation of doing so, but they are sadly remiss in the matter, and show a surprising negligence of their duty to me."

"A sort of criminal negligence," murmured Archer, and Stone grinned appreciatively. Miss Fordyce returned, and as she crossed the room, her pale green gown trailing, she came towards Stone with a rapt expression.

"I can help you," she said, "because I can evolve a mental picture of my friend, and project it to your mind by will-power."

"Pray don't trouble to do that, Miss Fordyce," said Stone, unable to keep a quizzical smile entirely suppressed. "You force me to confess that I have no knowledge of the occult, and depend entirely upon my own very practical common-sense and logic. What have you brought me?"

"A fan," answered Miss Fordyce, handing him one. "When I came up in the train this afternoon, a friend was with me during part of the journey. She lent me this fan, and I carelessly forgot to return it. As I know my friend very well, and you do not know her at all, it is a fair test."

"Fine!" said Anne Van Wyck, her intense eyes darkening with interest. "Beth, that is just the thing. Now, Mr. Stone, tell us of the fan's owner."

In her interest, Anne had moved nearer to Stone, and was breathlessly awaiting his words. The magnetic fascination of the woman is indescribable. I am positive that nothing on earth would have induced Fleming Stone to such an exhibition of his special powers of deduction, except Anne's compelling desire that he should.

I saw, too, though it was almost imperceptible, the effort Stone was obliged to make to detach his attention from her and concentrate it on the fan he was holding.

"To approach this matter in my usual way," he said quietly, "I shall have to ask permission to examine this fan under a magnifying glass. Have you one at hand?"

"Here is one," said Morland, bringing a fine one from his father's desk, at which action I fancied I saw a shade of annoyance pass over David Van Wyck's face.

For a few moments, Fleming Stone examined the fan through the glass.

In idle curiosity I looked at the faces of those grouped about. Mr. Van Wyck was clearly annoyed at the whole performance; though Morland, under the influence of Mrs. Stelton, waited in delighted anticipation. Condron Archer looked supercilious and even murmured to me that he doubted the detective's powers in such a test. Miss Fordyce wore the exalted air usual to people who affect the mystic. But Anne, the centre of the group, was surely enough to inspire Stone's latent powers to the utmost. She waited with a suppressed eagerness that seemed to show implicit faith in the result, and she even touched the fan as she too scanned it for any enlightening details.

Fleming Stone returned the glass to Morland and the fan to Miss Fordyce. But it was Anne whom he addressed.

"The fan," he said, in a quiet, narrative way, "belongs to a lady with dark hair and eyes and rosy cheeks, and a very perfect set of small, white teeth. She is healthy and rather robust, of a vigorous but not an athletic type. She is strong of muscle, but of rather a nervous temperament. She is thrifty and economical by nature, but proud and fastidious.   Usually of decorous habits, but likes occasionally a gayer experience. She is refined in her personal tastes and artistic in dressing, though fond of bright colors. She is kind and generous-hearted, unmarried, and past her first youth. She lives in or near the West Eighties in New York City, and her telephone

number has recently been changed to 9863 Schuyler. She
is fond of embroidering with colored silks, she possesses a
gown decorated with black spangled trimming, and she
wears a very heavy ring on the little finger of her right
hand." Stone finished as quietly as he had begun, but his
listeners were more excited.

"I don't believe a word of it!" Mrs. Stelton was saying,
and of course Morland agreed with her. But Beth Fordyce
was speaking, almost as if in a trance. "It is every word
true," she said, with a far-away look in her eyes. "If you
had known Leila, you could not have described her more
perfectly! Don't try to make me believe you are not occult!
You are positively clairvoyant!"

"Nonsense, Beth," said Anne impatiently. "Don't talk
such rubbish."

"No," said I; "occultism isn't in it with this kind of
work. Mr. Stone, that is the real thing. Are you going to
tell your processes of reasoning?"

"Of course he is!" cried Anne. "That will be the
delightful part of it. David, did you ever hear anything
like it?"

Though Anne turned her lovely flushed face toward
her husband, she received no answering smile.

"It doesn't interest me," he said coldly, and it is a
tribute to Anne's tact and cleverness that she quickly
covered this awkward speech by turning to Stone, saying
with utmost charm of manner, "Tell me all about it at
once. I can't wait another minute."

"My dear Mrs. Van Wyck," said Stone, seeming to
address her only, "I am very glad to explain, if it interests
you. You see, it's very simple, for this fan has been used a
good deal and naturally bears the impress of the lady who
has used it. To begin with, it is a souvenir fan that was
given to the lady when she dined in the restaurant of one
of the large hotels in New York. It is of the inexpensive
paper sort that is used for that purpose. But the name of
the restaurant has been carefully scratched out, showing
that the lady desired to keep and use it, but did not care

to have her friends know where she obtained it. This shows that the lady is not amply provided with fans, and shows too that she does not often frequent the gay restaurants. The fan is bright scarlet and gold, and, since she liked it well enough to keep it, I assume that it suited her brunette coloring, and also that she is fond of bright hues. She is nervous, because the fan shows that she has often picked at it—both its edge and its tassel—and has even frequently bitten it with her small, sharp teeth. You see, these lacquered sticks show clearly all marks and scratches, and this bar of metal that holds the tassel is much bent, showing a vigorous and healthy type. The fact that the fan has been used a great deal shows a robust and rosy-cheeked young woman, though not athletic, for athletic girls never use a fan. She is refined and fastidious in her tastes, for I notice a faint perfume of orris and violet. She is generous, for she gave away a fan that she found useful. And I think neither a very young girl nor a married lady would so long preserve a fan of this sort."

"But how did you know where she lives?" demanded Miss Fordyce.

"That argues a lack of observation on your part," said Stone, smiling. "On this light corner of the fan is written, though faintly, ' New No. 9863 Schuyler.' The people living in the vicinity of West Eighty-Third Street have recently had a change in their telephone-numbers; and when she noted a new number on her fan, I assumed it to be her own."

"It is," said Miss Fordyce. "But how did you know about her spangled dress and that curious ring she wears?"

"The ring left a decided impression on the outer sticks of the fan near the end, in such a position that it could come only from the abrasion of a heavy ring worn on the little finger. Then, you see, this tassel, as is usual on this sort of a fan, is of fine silk floss. It is much fluffed and tangled, and has a tendency to catch anything it may. In it I find a portion of a small black spangle, and two or three threads of fine embroidery floss, pink and green. Surely it is easy to infer that the lady uses embroidery silks frequently, and that the spangle is from one of her gowns."

"Don't take it so casually!" cried Anne, with an imperious nod at him. "You shall not so belittle your great powers. Supposing it is only logic and careful observation, no one else could do it! That fan could not have spoken to one of us, because our logic cannot understand its language. Mr. Stone, I thank you for doing that. I know you didn't want to."

"It isn't my custom to deduce for social entertainments," said Stone, smiling at her; "but it is my custom to accede to the wishes of my hostess."

"Thank you for that, then;" and Anne smiled back at him. "Now, as a small return favor, may I show you over the house? Mrs. Davidson tells me you want to see it."

"Yes, I'm interested. I understand it is very old and was built by an eccentric."

"Yes, it was; though we bought it from its second owner. Mr. Sturgis, will you go with us?"

I was glad to accept the invitation, and as we started we were joined by Miss Fordyce and Archer, and also by Mrs. Stelton and Morland Van Wyck. So it was quite a party which followed Anne through the doorway in the corner.

We found ourselves in a corridor that ran along the south side of the house. We passed a branch corridor bearing to the right, but Anne laughingly remarked that those were the apartments of herself and her husband, and we might not enter. We went on into a beautiful music-room, through stately reception and drawing-rooms, and into a delightful library. There were billiard and smoking-rooms near by, and through the dining-room and sunny breakfast-room we passed out to the terrace and down into the gardens. I thought Stone seemed disappointed that, though the house was old, it gave no hint of secret passages or dark staircases. No dungeons or anything that savored of mystery or crime. I chanced to be walking by his side, and I rallied him on this.

"It is so," he confessed. "From what I had heard of the house, I had fancied it more complicated in structure. It is very four-square."

"Yes, it is," said I, as we looked at it from across the wide expanse of lawn and garden.

"Curious construction, though," mused Stone, "and yet perfectly simple: one large rectangle, with smaller rectangles attached at its two back corners."

"Usually wings are built entirely across the ends," I observed.

"Oh, of course it was done to get the advantage of light. Wings at the ends would have darkened many of the rooms; but attached so, at the corners, there are windows all round each part of the house."

This was true, and, as I now recollected, every room was flooded with daylight.

"I must join my hostess now," said Stone, "and make my adieux. I am leaving to-night for Kansas City, where I'm about to investigate a most important case."

I longed to ask him about it, but I didn't feel privileged to do so. I did, however, express my pleasure in knowing him, and hoped that we might meet again. He very courteously gave me his card, bearing an address that he said would always reach him; an attention that I prized highly, though it might never fulfil its purpose.

We all returned to the study, and after the departure of the Davidsons and their distinguished friend, the talk naturally turned to Fleming Stone and his work. "It's uncanny, that's what it is," declared Mr. Van Wyck, "and it gives me the fidgets to have the man around."

"I feel that way, too," said Connie Archer. "Why, I'm perfectly sure that he could see straight through my coat into my pocket and read a letter there that I wouldn't have anybody know about— not anybody!"

"Is it one I wrote you?" asked Anne, so roguishly that it was most apparent fooling, but her husband looked up and scowled.

"Yes," returned Archer, with a most obvious intent of teasing his host; "that last delightful missive of yours!"

At this, David Van Wyck frowned angrily, and Anne said, "Nonsense, Connie, such jokes aren't funny. What is the letter about, really?"

"It's a tailor's dun," said Archer, taking his cue; "but I wouldn't have Stone know it for anything. I expect he pays his bills before they're due."

"Of course he does," said Morland: "deduces the exact amount they're going to be, and sends off a check without seeing 'em."

"Well, don't ask him here again, Anne," said her husband. "I don't like him."

"He won't come again very soon," I volunteered. "He's off to-night for Kansas City."

"Good thing, too," growled Mr. Van Wyck.

"And now you people may seek some other pasture. I expect some callers to-night, and I want to get this place into some semblance of a gentleman's study, instead of a picnic ground."

"Oh, David," said his wife, "are they coming to-night?"

"Yes, they are. My mind is made up, Anne, and I'd rather you wouldn't refer to the subject."

"It's an outrage!" said Morland, under his breath. He spoke to Anne, but his father heard it, and said, "None of that, boy! I suppose I have a right to do as I choose with my own! And if you know when you're well off, you'll accept the situation gracefully. It'll be better for you in the long run."

Morland turned away, looking obstinate and sullen. I had no idea what it was all about, but when I looked at Anne her face was so tragic in its utter despair that I was startled. Surely I had been right in thinking her light-hearted manner was a cloak for some desperate, heart-breaking trouble. But in obedience to Mr. Van Wyck's

command, we all left the study. It was not quite time to
dress for dinner, so we strolled out through the great
doors onto the terrace; and even as we left, the footmen
were already clearing away the tea-things.

Chapter 4: The Decision Of David Van Wyck

FROM a certain terrace-landing which Anne called her "Sunset View," we watched the last glowing clouds dull and darken in the west. A sort of depression had fallen on the party, because—as was perfectly evident—of Anne's mood. She was distrait and preoccupied; though now and then her dark eyes flashed with what was unmistakably anger.

"What's it all about, Anne dear?" said Archer, who let himself go a little when Mr. Van Wyck wasn't present.

Instead of evading or parrying his question, Anne spoke out frankly.

"It's just this," she said: "David is going to give away all his fortune. He's going to build and endow a magnificent library for Crescent Falls Village—a library out of all proportion to a tiny little place like this."

"All his fortune!" I exclaimed, astounded.

"You can't mean that, Anne!"

"But I do mean just that! He calls it philanthropy—that's his fad this year. If he were really philanthropic, it would be different; but he has become deeply absorbed in this ridiculous hobby for no reason at all except that he's always dashing into some new and crazy scheme. And he's so determined; he'll give away all his money, and then afterward he'll be sorry, but he can't get it back. He has had fads and foibles before, but though sometimes they were trying, they never involved such an amount of money as this."

"But, Anne," I went on, "you can't mean that he's going to give away all his money! How will he provide for you and his two children?"

"He says I've got to strike out for myself," growled Morland, who had been listening moodily, as with his hands in his pockets he leaned against the terrace-rail.

"Well, he's going to give nearly a million to the library," said Anne despondently; "and that's just about all he possesses. He says it's right to practise philanthropy and give away one's fortune while one's alive."

"Other good and great men have pursued that same plan," said Beth Fordyce, with one of her exalted looks.

"Yes," spoke up Barbara Van Wyck angrily; "but the other good and great men had many millions to start with. Father's going to give away all he has, except just enough for us to live on in a very small way. It isn't fair to us, and he has no right to do it, but he is simply immovable in the matter."

"I feel as Anne does," said Archer seriously.

"If it were real, true philanthropy, it would be a noble deed; but I know Mr. Van Wyck, and he is always rushing suddenly and madly into some new project, which he as quickly abandons and regrets."

"Ah, Connie," said Anne, "if there were only a hope of his abandoning this! But when he regrets it, it will be too late."

"Yes, the committee-men are coming to-night, for the final acceptance of the deed of gift, or whatever you call it," said Barbara, in a tone of blended rage and despair.

I had thought Barbara Van Wyck was colorless, but in the intensity of her feelings her eyes flashed and the red rose to her pale cheeks until she looked like a veritable avenging angel. I hadn't known she possessed so much energy, and I turned to her, saying hopefully, "Can't you persuade your father, at least, to delay it?"

"No; I've tried every argument I know of, and so have Morland and Anne. If Anne can't persuade him, nobody can."

Though this praise was grudgingly given, it was unmistakably earnest; and it was clear to be seen that, though Anne and her step-children were not congenial, and not even friendly, they had common cause in this impending catastrophe.

And I could not blame them. Such ill-advised and misplaced generosity was absurd, and seemed to me to argue Mr. Van Wyck's mind somewhat unbalanced. But as a comparative stranger, I didn't like to offer suggestions, or even comment very emphatically.

Mrs. Stelton, however, felt no such restraint.

"It's outrageous!" she cried. "It's contemptible! I never heard of such a performance! If I were you, Morland, I should have my father adjudged insane."

"He is insane on that subject," muttered Morland; "but what can I do about it? If you knew my father as I do, you'd know that, insane or not, he will have his own way."

"Yes, he will," said Anne, sighing, and looking so adorably pathetic that it didn't seem possible any one could disappoint her as Van Wyck proposed to do.

"Won't he listen to you, Anne?" I asked. "Doesn't he care for your comfort and happiness?"

"No," said Anne, and though she looked the picture of utter hopelessness, she showed also a cool reserve that warned me not to intrude too far upon her personal affairs.

"Of course he cares for Anne," broke in Archer; "but I tell you, he's out of his head! He doesn't know what he's doing."

"He isn't out of his head, Connie," returned Anne gently, "and he does know what he's doing. I'm going to try once more, before the committee comes, to make him change his mind, but I haven't much hope. Come, people, we must go and dress for dinner."

Archer threw discretion to the winds and gazed frankly at Anne, as he said, "How can he refuse you anything? No man could, I know!"

Anne, though her color rose a little, didn't even glance at Archer, but, turning to me, walked by my side toward the house, chatting lightly on trivial subjects.

Later, as we gathered around the dinner-table, one could scarcely believe there was such an undercurrent of trouble among the Van Wycks. Our host was unusually bland and affable, Barbara was placid, and Morland was the debonair man of the world that society requires.

As to Anne, she was a marvel. In a dinner gown of pale yellow satin, which suited especially well her exquisite coloring, her wonderful hair coiled low, and her great eyes shining, she seemed animated by some unusual energy. She was roguish and dictatorial by turns. She was dignified one moment and softly pathetic the next. I couldn't make her out. Either she had persuaded her husband to abandon his plan, or the matter was still undecided. At any rate, she could not have tried and failed, and still have shown this vivacity. But I did not yet know my Anne. I sat next her, and dinner was not half over before she confided to me the news of her total failure.

"Not only did David refuse to listen to me," she said, "but he forbade me to speak to him again on the subject; and he spoke to me in such a way and in such language that I can never forgive him."

"Anne!" I exclaimed, for, though smiling, her smile was assumed for the others' benefit; and her low tones, heard only by me, were full of bitterness and desperate grief.

"Anne," I murmured involuntarily, "let me help you. What can I do?"

"Nothing," she replied. "No one can help me."

Perhaps it was the pathos of the situation, perhaps it was her marvellous beauty, enhanced by the dramatic moment, or perhaps it was inevitable, but I fell in love with Anne Van Wyck then and there. Or, rather, it was an awakening to the fact that I had always loved her, even when we were schooltime friends. Naturally, I had sufficient self-control not to disclose this secret even by a glance, but repeated in carefully modulated tones my desire and willingness to help her, if possible; and then, with an effort, I turned to talk to my neighbor on the other side. It proved to be Beth Fordyce, and her pale blue eyes lighted as she began to talk eagerly to me.

"Let us make a pact, Mr. Sturgis," she said. "I, too, want to help Anne, and surely together we can do something."

It was quite evident that she had overheard my words, and this annoyed me; and I answered that, with all the willingness in the world, I failed to see how Mrs. Van Wyck's guests could do anything in this matter. She took the hint, and changed the subject, but almost immediately after Mrs. Stelton's shrill voice was heard addressing the table at large.

"Well, I think you're perfectly horrid, Mr. Van Wyck!" she exclaimed, shaking a beringed hand at him. "To give away all that lovely money that ought to belong to Anne and Barbie and Mr. Morland!" The last name was accompanied by a coquettish glance in Morland's direction, but she went on, addressing her host: "Why, if a husband of mine did that, I'd—I'd shut him up on bread and water for a week!"

"Perhaps he would enjoy the rest, Mrs. Stelton," said Van Wyck, gazing at her blandly. The man had a way of saying these things, which, though rude, was rather enjoyable to disinterested hearers.

Good-natured Mrs. Stelton laughed. "Oh, what waggery!" she cried. "But if it brought him to his senses, I shouldn't mind. I've a notion to shut you up for a week, Mr. Van Wyck, and let you think this matter over!"

"Though I always enjoy your witty chat, my dear Mrs. Stelton, I must beg of you to drop this subject;" and this time Mr. Van Wyck's air of finality brought us a respite from Mrs. Stelton's silly observations. But Morland gave one parting shaft.

"If you do this thing, Dad," he growled, "you'll be mighty sorry!"

A silence fell. It was not so much what Morland said, but the quiet intensity of his tone, which seemed to convey a definite threat. Indeed, his father must have felt it, for he looked up quickly at his son; but he only said sarcastically, "I thank you for your warning," and then the subject really was dropped.

Anne resumed her gayety, though I now knew for a certainty it was all a pretense. Con Archer nobly helped her out, and chatted lightly and gracefully. Barbara continued to sulk in silence, but all the rest rose to the occasion, and only appropriate dinner-table talk was heard.

Coffee was served in the drawing-room for the ladies, while the men remained at table. Perhaps from a sense of duty, Archer made one more effort.

"I say, Van Wyck," he began, "I know it's none of my business, but mayn't I suggest as man to man, that you think this matter over a bit longer before making your decision? You know, to a disinterested observer, the gift you propose to make seems out of all proportion to its object; and I can't help thinking that on second thoughts you would agree to this yourself."

"Mr. Archer," said Van Wyck coldly, "the only one of your remarks to which I agree is your first one: that it is none of your business."

Condron Archer flushed, but as David Van Wyck's guests were not unusued to his scathing speeches, this one was not openly resented; and Archer said nothing further.

And then, seemingly unable to control himself, Morland blurted out, "I say, Dad, you just can't do it!"

"Can't?" and the elder Van Wyck raised his eyebrows at his son.

"No, can't!" Morland went on, blindly angry now. "It's heathenish! It's a crime against your wife and daughter, to say nothing of me. I tell you, you can't!"

David Van Wyck's clear, cutting tones fell like icicles: "If you will be present, Morland, at the meeting this evening, I shall take pleasure in showing you that I can."

"You bet I'll be there!" and Morland looked almost like a belligerent boy as he met the cold stare of his father's eyes.

"I'm glad you accept my invitation; and now shall we join the ladies—?" Rising from the table, we crossed the hall to the drawing-room; and perhaps four angrier men never wore the smiling mask of politeness.

Anne, seated in a carved, high-backed chair, made an exquisite picture, and she turned her beautiful, appealing eyes to her husband as he entered. David Van Wyck crossed the room straight to her. Placing his hands on the two carved griffins' heads that formed the arms of the chair, he leaned over the beautiful face upturned to his, and whispered a few words in Anne's ear. Then he lightly kissed her on the cheek, and, without a word to any one else, strolled out of the room toward the study.

What he said to her nobody knew, but Anne turned deathly white, and grasped the carved chairarms as if in extremest agony. I was uncertain whether to notice this and go to her assistance, or whether to keep up the farce of gay conversation in an endeavor to cover her agitation.

Morland gave his step-mother one glance, clenched his teeth, and, muttering, "Brute!" strode off after his father.

Without hesitation, Archer drew a chair to Anne's side, and, sitting down, took her hand in his. But he erred, for Anne drew away her hand with a freezing dignity, and, rising, came over and sat by Mrs. Stelton.

And then I was surprised by another of Anne's absolutely inexplicable changes of mood. "What a heavenly brooch!" she said, smiling at Mrs. Stelton. "Florentine work, isn't it? I perfectly adore those things! I have one something like it, but a more conventional design. Don't you just love to buy things in Florence, or in Naples, or indeed any part of Italy? Italy is lovely, isn't it?" Mrs. Stelton stared at this flow of insane talk, and I suddenly wondered if Anne were hysterical. I saw Archer move as if to approach her and then turn on his heel again, doubtless fearing rebuff. So I dared to venture, myself. "Mrs. Van Wyck," I said, "won't you come with me for a little walk on the terrace? I'm sure the cool air will be refreshing."

"Thank you," said Anne simply, and she went with me at once, draping the long train of her gown over her arm as we passed through the hall.

"You are very good," she said, a little wearily, as we stepped out onto the terrace. "How did you know I wanted to get away?"

I stifled an impulse to tell her that love helped me to read her thoughts, and said quietly, "I know you're troubled about that plan of your husband's, but let us hope for the best."

"There is no longer room for hope," she said dully. "Come, let us look in at the window."

Of course I followed her along the terrace to the windows of the great study. We could easily look in, and the deep colors of the stained glass prevented our being seen by those inside. And, any way, there was surely no harm in it. We saw Mr. Van Wyck and Morland, and three other men, who doubtless represented the committee.

"Yes," murmured Anne musingly; "there they are. Mr. Millar, Mr. Brandt, and Mr. Garson. I do not blame them. Of course, if David offers them this money, they'd be foolish not to take it. Mr. Brandt is the only one who has really over-urged in the matter. In fact, he suggested it to David first. Oh, Raymond, isn't it too bad!"

It was the first time she had called me by my first name, and I felt a thrill that blotted out all thought of Van Wyck or his money.

"And you mustn't think," she went on, "that I'm selfish or ungenerous. If David were honestly a philanthropist, or if I weren't so sure that he'd regret this later, as he does all his erratic impulses, I'd feel different about it. But you see how it is, don't you, Raymond?"

"Yes, Anne, I see how it is." And though I spoke quietly, my heart was in a tumult.

"Oh, look!" she cried. "Morland is getting angry! He is quarrelling with his father!"

"Don't be alarmed," I said. "Morland can never get the better of that man. His father will not mind anything he says."

But it was evident that Morland had said something that his father did mind, for the elder man's temper was roused, and the two were certainly in deadly earnest. We could hear no word that was spoken, but the three visitors looked appalled, and were evidently trying to pacify the combatants.

"Come away, Anne," I said, sick at heart over the whole matter. "You can do nothing—why torture yourself by looking on? Let me tell you what I brought you for a gift."

"What?" she asked, but without interest. I led her back across the terrace, as I told her of a beautiful piece of Venetian glass that I had brought for her. It was a gem, rare and valuable, but I would not have lauded it as I did except in an endeavor to distract her mind from the sight she had just seen.

"Where is it?" she asked, at last, faintly interested.

"I gave it to a footman when I came," I replied.

"Then he will have given it to my maid, and it will be in my room," she said; then, hesitatingly, "Don't think it strange, will you, if—if I don't tell David that you gave it to me? He is—he is peculiar, you know."

"Jealous, you mean," I said, laughing. "That doesn't surprise me, and, truly, I'm glad of the fact that I can make him jealous!"

But I'm not sure that Anne heard this, so preoccupied was she with her own thoughts. We returned to the drawing-room, but it was not long before we all went to our rooms.

Anne bade me good-night on the stair-landing. "David and Morland are still shut up with that committee," she said; "and I am going at once in search of the gift you brought me. I know I shall love it "

"For the sake of the giver," I interrupted, with a gay foolery that sounded as if I didn't mean it; but I did.

"Not at all," said Anne saucily. "I shall love it only for its beauty and intrinsic worth. And if it's Venetian glass, it must have both. I hope to goodness it isn't smashed!"

"I think not; I had it packed carefully. Goodnight, Anne."

"Good-night," she said, her long lashes sweeping her cheeks; and then added, as an afterthought, "Raymond."

And as she disappeared, I wondered whether she had spoken my name from pure coquetry, or—what?

CHAPTER 5: THE CRIME IN THE STUDY

THERE are few things, to my mind, more delightful than being wakened soon after daybreak, on a perfect spring morning, by the songs of birds. As I was thus brought to my senses, it took me a moment to realize just where I was, but a glance from my window reminded me.

I sprang up and threw aside the curtains, and revelled in the flowery breath of the morning air. Again, the view enchanted me. The distant hills, the nearer rolling fields and bits of woods, and closer yet, the wonderful park that surrounded the home of the Van Wycks.

Surely, I thought, Anne Mansfield was justified in marrying for a home, when one considered the home.

And that that was Anne's reason for accepting David Van Wyck, I hadn't the slightest doubt. Anne had been uncomfortably poor, as a girl, and I knew how she had always craved luxurious surroundings.

I didn't for a moment believe she loved her husband. But I knew her well enough to be sure that her sense of honor and loyalty would keep her a true and devoted wife to him. If she flirted with Archer,—if she even coquetted with me,—it was only the natural amusement of a beautiful woman, who was frankly fond of admiration. And thus I made excuses for her, as I stood looking out of my East window, and the sun grew more and more dazzling in its early morning splendor.

Beneath me spread the beautiful lawn, that would have done credit to an English ancestral castle. Here and there, I saw a gardener or other servant moving about, and I concluded the place was under good discipline. I looked backward to the East wing. Since I had been inside the study, I could judge better of its noble proportions and impressive lines. Yet, it looked forbidding. Not exactly sinister, but grim and rather awesome.

The long, narrow windows gave it a gloomy air, and as there was no entrance visible from where I looked, it seemed almost like a prison. Ivy trailed over its casements, and the birds flew in and out of the vines, twittering. It was really too early to dress and go downstairs, but I suddenly became possessed of a wild hope that Anne might be in the habit of strolling in the gardens before breakfast. I had not the least reason to suppose this, but a strange impatience urged me to go down and see. So, completing a leisurely toilet, I went downstairs, and through the great hall to the front door. A parlor-maid, who was dusting about, opened the door for me, and though I thought an expression of surprise showed for a moment on her face, she quickly suppressed it.

I stepped out into the beautiful morning, with a feeling of gladness that I had come down, even if I were doomed to solitude. I saw no sign of Anne, nor of any one else, save a few caretakers, and I started off for a long ramble through the grounds. Their interest and beauty well repaid me, and as I returned toward the house, I sat down upon a stone seat overlooking a picturesque ravine. Not far away, I could see the stables and garage, but there was no one stirring in their vicinity.

"Late risers, here," I thought to myself, surprised that the stablemen should not yet be about. And then I saw a woman peering in at the window of one of the buildings. My heart gave a leap, hoping that it might be Anne, but it was not. I saw, in a moment, that it was the housekeeper, Mrs. Carstairs.

She wore a smart white linen morning gown, so trig of appearance that she looked like some Parisienne dressed for an outing. The skirt was short, showing dainty white shoes and stockings, and altogather, she looked as little like an English housekeeper as could be imagined.

And then I recollected, no one had told me she was English. The valet had been called so, and doubtless his father was an Englishman, but this mysterious mother of his was certainly French, or I never saw a Frenchwoman. Then my musing concerning her nationality gave way to an interest in her present occupation,—for, surely, she was acting strangely. She went round the garage, peering in at each window; now and then casting furtive glances, as if in fear of being observed. She could not see me, as I was hidden by some foliage plants. Then, leaving the garage, she walked back along the driveway toward the house, her eyes on the ground, as if looking for something.

Natural chivalry prompting me to assist her, I rose and walked rapidly toward her.

"May I help in your search, Mrs. Carstairs?" I said, in my most Chesterfieldian tones.

Apparently she had not heard my approach, for she turned as if greatly startled, and said, fairly gasping for breath:

"Oh,—oh; I thought you were—you—were some one else!"

"No, I'm myself," I said, smiling, for we had met, for a few moments the evening before, and I was not at all unwilling to speak to her again.

"Have you lost something?"

"Only my self-possession," she returned, with such apt repartee, that I said, impulsively, "You are French, aren't you?"

"Partly," she replied, looking at me in surprise at my evident interest in the matter.

"And you haven't lost anything else,—not so easily replaced?"

She caught my allusion and smiled; then, as if recollecting herself, she assumed a severely correct manner, and said: "No, thank you. I have lost nothing."

"But you've been studying the ground all the way from the garage."

She turned on me like a fury.

"Nothing of the sort!" she exclaimed, with flashing eyes. "How dare you say so? Why should I study the ground?"

"Good Heavens!" I cried; "it isn't a crime to study the ground, is it? Why shouldn't you, if you choose to?"

"I don't choose to! I have no interest in the ground. I was—I was looking at the sky!"

"I won't contradict you," I said, politely, though aghast at this whopper. "Have you, perhaps, lost something in the sky, then? or —"

"Yes; a couple of Pleiads," she replied, with an irrepressible laugh, and I marvelled afresh to hear a housekeeper talk in this strain.

"I am certainly destined to get no 'Lost and Found Information,'" I said, though uncertain as to whether I ought to talk to her in this companionable way.

"Are you out for information this morning?"

"I'm really out to see if the Poets sing true about the delights of early rising. But I'm always glad to absorb information if it comes in my way."

"Do you want it on any especial subject?"

"Yes," I returned, daringly. "I want to know why you detest Mrs. Van Wyck so intensely."

It was interesting to watch Mrs. Carstairs's face after this. First, she gave me a stare of blank amazement; then, a flash of indignation burst from her stormy eyes; then, like a ray of sunlight, she smiled sweetly, and said: "I don't detest her; I adore her!"

And then she turned from me, and walked swiftly down a by-path.

I looked after her. She walked beautifully, without haste, but with a rapid, graceful movement. I knew perfectly well she had told me an untruth. She did detest Anne, and she had chosen a most clever way to deny it, and to close the conversation at the same time.

The path she took led toward the kitchen quarters, and she soon disappeared inside, while I went on, across the terrace and in at the rear door of the great hall. A footman showed me to the breakfast-room; a cheery, sunny place, much cosier than the big room where we had dined the night before. I followed him, with a comfortable sense of having a healthy, hearty appetite.

When I entered the breakfast-room Archer and Morland Van Wyck were already at the table. The ladies, Morland informed me, breakfasted in their own rooms.

"And your father?" I asked, as I seated myself.

"Oh, Dad's usually the earliest bird about. His interview with that precious committee last night must have worn him out, and he's sleeping late."

"Then, the committee succeeded in their fell design?" asked Archer.

"Yes, they succeeded, but you mustn't say fell design. Dad was in no way coerced by those men. In fact, he—"

"He coerced them to take his money?" I asked, smiling.

"Not quite that," returned Morland; "but they were very fair about it. They put it to him squarely that he was doing injustice to his family by such a gift. You know what Dad is. The more they objected, the more determined he was to have his way."

"If they had seemed eager for the money," observed Archer, "Mr. Van Wyck might have reconsidered."

"Exactly that," agreed Morland. "Father's very perversity made him insist on carrying out his plan. So, he made out a deed of gift, and though the whole matter wasn't entirely settled up, yet it is practically decided, and we Van Wycks are no longer rich people."

"It's an outrage!" I cried, thinking of Anne's deprivation. "Is Mr. Van Wyck a Socialist?"

"Oh, no," said Morland; "not a bit of that. Mrs. Carstairs is the only Socialist in this household. Father's idea is philanthropy,—and he suddenly took a notion that the time to practise that, is during one's lifetime, and not by a will."

"Is Mrs. Carstairs a Socialist?" I inquired, my mind going back to her strange, almost weird personality.

"She's everything that's queer," said Morland, with a grim smile. "I don't profess to understand her. But I do know she has some peculiar influence over my father. I'm not sure she persuaded him to give this Library to the town, but I know she had a hand in it."

"Why should she want him to do such a thing?" I asked in surprise.

Morland glanced about, and as there seemed to be no servant in hearing, he said, in a low voice:

"She hates Anne, and she wants Dad's money to go anywhere, rather than to his family."

"Does she hate the rest of you?" I asked, in a whisper.

"She's indifferent to Barb and me. But she's actively hostile to Anne. Of course the presumption is, that she hoped to catch Dad in her own net, and failing, resented his marriage to another woman."

"She doesn't seem to show any especial interest in your father," commented Archer.

"You can't judge," Morland said. "She's a deep one; I never saw such a woman. She must be over forty, and she looks like a girl. I steer clear of her always. She's too many for me."

"She certainly has a strange manner," I began, and then paused, as I heard a step behind me. "Morland," said a low voice from the hall, and I looked up to see Anne standing in the doorway.

She wore a rose-colored boudoir gown and a lacy cap. She was pale, and her small white hand grasped nervously at the portiere.

"What is it, Anne?" said Morland, as we all rose.

"Your father—he—he hasn't been in his room all night. He's locked in the study, and Carstairs can't get in."

Carstairs, the young English valet, was behind Anne, and, though his expression was the conventional blank, his face was white and his eyes showed a vague fear.

"Whew!" exclaimed Morland. "Stayed in there all night! Must have fallen asleep after his committee meeting."

"But Carstairs has pounded on the door, and I've called and called," said Anne, nervously. "Won't you come?"

Morland went at once, and Archer and I hesitatingly followed.

We paused as we passed through the drawingroom, but then, hearing Morland's loud calls, with apparently no response, we went on through the corridor that led to the study.

"Nothing doing," said Morland, as we approached; and though his tone was light, I saw that he was seriously alarmed.

"Can't we get in the other door?" I suggested; and Archer added, "Or a window?"

"Not through the windows, sir," said Carstairs. "They're all fastened inside."

"The outside door, then," said I, and Archer followed me as we went back through the corridor, out on the terrace, and tried to open the massive doors of the study. But we might as well have attempted to enter a locked cathedral. We tried to peer in at the windows, but the inner blinds were drawn, and we could see nothing. We returned to the house, where Anne and Morland were still endeavoring to get a response to their repeated calls.

"Looks queer," said Morland, shaking his head. "I'm afraid old Dad has had a stroke or something."

His tone seemed to me altogether too careless for the possibility he was suggesting, but my interest and attention were centred on Anne. She was trembling violently, her face was white and drawn, and her eyes had a haunted look, as of a terrible fear.

"We must get in," she whispered. "Something must have happened."

"Shall we break down the door?" I asked.

"Impossible," said Archer. "I doubt if six men could break in that door."

"That's right," said Morland. "These old doors are not the flimsy sort they make nowadays. We must pick the lock. Carstairs, go for Ranney, the garage mechanician. He can manage it. Tell him to bring tools."

The valet made a queer, unintelligible sound in his throat, and trembling greatly, leaned against the wall.

"I—c-can't, sir," he said, and really, the man seemed on the verge of collapse.

"What!" cried Morland; "you must! No nonsense! Go at once for Ranney."

"I'll go," I volunteered, for Carstairs was positively unable to move.

I ran to the garage and called Ranney, making as little fuss as possible, for I didn't want a panic among the stablemen. I felt sure that David Van Wyck had suffered an apoplectic or paralytic stroke, and the immediate necessity was to get to him.

"What is it, sir?" said Ranney, touching his cap as he came forward.

"Bring some tools," I said, "to force open a locked door. And then, come on to the study, with no questions."

"Very good, sir."

In a moment I had rejoined the group of people clustered at the study door.

"I wish you would go to your room, Anne," Archer was saying, gently. "I'm sure it would be better."

"Yes, do," said Morland. "Where's your maid? . . . Here, Jeannette!"

And as the frightened maid appeared, Morland said, "Take care of Mrs. Van Wyck. Take her to her room, stay with her, and don't chatter to her."

The suite of rooms occupied by Anne and her husband were close at hand, and as maid and mistress disappeared, Ranney came.

"Get to work and open that door," ordered Morland. "Pick the lock or cut it out, whichever is necessary, but get us in."

Ranney picked the lock skilfully and rapidly, but still the door refused to open. "It's bolted," he said.

"Cut out the bolt," said Morland, on whom the suspense was beginning to tell.

Ranney obeyed, and, though marring and spoiling the beautiful door, he succeeded at last in throwing it back on its hinges, and we went in.

David Van Wyck sat in his desk chair, motionless, with a stain of blood on his shirt-front and waistcoat.

"Murdered!" exclaimed Morland, springing forward. "By some of that blamed committee! I'll be revenged for this!" As he spoke, he was feeling for his father's heart and pulse, though there was no possible doubt that the man was dead.

As we all stood in horror-stricken silence, my mind worked rapidly. "Hold on, Morland," I said. "It can't be murder, with this room locked up as it was. Your father did this himself."

Morland turned from his father and stared at me. "Suicide!" he exclaimed. "Absurd! Why should Dad want to kill himself?"

"I don't know, I'm sure," I replied; "but as we couldn't get into this locked room, how could a murderer have done so?"

"I tell you it was one of that committee," declared Morland. "My father had no reason and no desire to kill himself!"

"As to that," put in Archer, "why should those men of the committee want to kill him? He was about to give them his money. And, as Sturgis says, no one could have murdered him and got away, leaving this room entirely locked on the inside. But something ought to be done. You ought to send for a—a doctor or something."

"What good could a doctor do now!" said Morland, looking a little dazed. "But I suppose it is the right thing to do. Carstairs, telephone for Doctor Mason and tell him to come at once. Don't tell him what for—there's no use of this getting all over until we know something more about it ourselves. Use this telephone here on the desk."

With difficulty, Carstairs controlled himself sufficiently to obey orders. Morland strode about the room. "It's so," he declared. "Every window is fastened with these enormous bolts, that are more than burglar-proof. And this outside door, as you see, is bolted like a barricade. There is no other possible entrance except the door at which we came in, and you all know how secure that was. Consequently, it must be that my father killed himself. But why should he?"

"And how did he do it?" said I, suddenly realizing that there was no weapon lying about.

"I don't know—don't ask me!" and with a groan Morland flung himself into a chair and buried his face in his hands. He seemed like a man who had utterly collapsed after passing through a terrible ordeal, and I said to Archer, "Let's leave him alone, and do what we can ourselves."

"What can we do?" said Archer. "We mustn't touch anything, you know, until the coroner comes."

"Coroner!" I exclaimed. "Good gracious, does he have to come?"

"Isn't he always called, in case of a mysterious death?"

"Well, this is certainly a mysterious death, if ever there was one," I declared; "but I don't believe that, about not touching anything until the coroner gets here. I've heard it's a mistaken notion."

"Well, do as you like, on your own responsibility," said Archer; "if you think you can discover a clue to the mystery, go ahead."

CHAPTER 6: SURMISES

BUT I could discover nothing, except to confirm the fact that there was no possible way for an intruder to have left that room locked up as it was; and that consequently it must have been either accident or intentional self-destruction.

But I looked in vain for a weapon. There was no revolver on the desk or on the floor, near the dead man. I scrutinized carefully the soft, thick rug, and was rewarded at last by finding a clue.

Without disturbing Morland, who still sat, with hidden face, I went near to Archer, and spoke in a low voice.

"At any rate, I know what killed him."

"What?" and Archer looked amazed.

"He was shot," I said, trying to hide my pride in my own discovery.

"How do you know?"

"Look on the floor. There, near his chair, are five or six small shot. See them?"

Archer stared at the floor and saw the shot almost at Van Wyck's very feet.

"But how on earth " he began, when Doctor Mason came into the room.

His professional calm a little upset by this tragedy, the doctor's hand trembled as he examined the body of David Van Wyck.

It took but a few moments, for the red stain on the white shirt bosom told its own story.

"Suicide?" he inquired, as he completed his task.

"Must have been," said Archer, "as he was locked in here alone. How was he killed? What is the wound?"

"I don't know," said Doctor Mason, looking puzzled. "He may have been shot by a very small calibre pistol, or he may have been stabbed by some sharp instrument. You see, this small hole in his shirt-bosom is perfectly round; but there are no powder-marks."

I called the doctor's attention to the shot on the floor, and he looked more puzzled still. "But he wasn't shot with a shotgun," he said. "In fact, I incline to the opinion that he was stabbed with some sharp, round instrument."

"A hat-pin," I suggested.

"No," said the doctor impatiently; "there isn't one hat-pin out of a hundred made that could go through a stiff shirt-bosom without bending. But something like that, only rather thicker. You see the size of the hole."

"But mayn't it be a bullet-hole?" said Archer.

"It may be. At any rate, we must send for the coroner. Wake up, Morland." The doctor had crossed the room and laid his hand not unkindly on Morland Van Wyck's shoulder. He shook him slightly, and Morland raised his white, drawn face.

"Must we have the coroner?" he asked. "Can't we call it a stroke or something, and not have any publicity? It's going to be awful hard on—on Anne."

Something in his tone made me realize Morland's feeling for his father's beautiful young wife. Doubtless he had concealed and even tried to overcome it, but now in his hour of trial his first thoughts flew to her. This explained to my mind his sudden collapse after his earlier attitude of bravado. I had thought he resented his father's second marriage, but now I believed that he himself had succumbed to Anne's irresistible fascination. I, too, felt it would be desirable to spare Anne the horrors of publicity, if possible, so I said:

"Can the matter be hushed up, and made to appear an accident or a natural death?"

"No," said Dr. Mason bluntly. "I could not give my professional sanction to any such course. And I think Mrs. Van Wyck should be told of this matter at once."

Just then Anne came into the study. She had seen Doctor Mason arrive, and considered it her right to know what had happened to her husband. She wore a simple morning-gown, and her maid Jeannette hovered behind her with a vinaigrette of smelling-salts.

"What has happened?" said Anne, advancing steadily into the room. And then, as she saw the still figure of David Van Wyck, she looked at each of us in turn. Seeming to make a choice, she went to Doctor Mason, and, putting her hands on his arm, said simply, "Tell me."

"Mrs. Van Wyck," said the old doctor, straightforwardly, "your husband is dead. We do not know exactly the means of his death, and I'm afraid it will be necessary to put the matter into the hands of the coroner."

Anne's slender figure swayed a little, but she did not faint, and Doctor Mason gently steadied her, as he went on talking: "There is nothing you can do, Mrs. Van Wyck, and as your physician, I advise you to go to your room and lie down."

"No, I will not go to my room and lie down," Anne declared; "who killed my husband?"

She was strangely calm,—so calm, that I knew she was straining every nerve to preserve her poise, and I feared her sudden breakdown.

"That is yet to be discovered," said Doctor Mason; "if, indeed, we do not find out that he took his own life."

"He did not do that," said Anne; "he never would do that!"

Her voice was almost inaudible, and her face was white as death. She still clutched the old doctor's arm, as if unable to stand alone.

We three men stood, looking at her. I felt sure all three loved her; Archer, Moreland and I. It was a strange situation, for a subtle sense told me that we all wanted to go to her assistance, but none dared do so. We seemed, almost, to be waiting, till she should make a choice of one of us.

But she did not heed us. Addressing herself entirely to the doctor, she rambled on, not hysterically, but with a far-away look, as if only half-conscious of what she was saying.

"No; David would not commit suicide,—of that, I am sure. Somebody killed him,—murdered him,—but who? Could it have been--" her voice died away in an unintelligible murmur, and she fainted.

Doctor Mason held her in his arms, as we all sprang forward.

"Morland," said the doctor, making his own choice, "help me carry Mrs. Van Wyck to her room. Where is her maid?"

They took Anne away, and I turned to Archer.

"Her bedroom is on this floor?" I asked.

"Yes; Van Wyck used to have his rooms on the second floor. But when he married his present wife, he had a magnificent suite of apartments furnished for them on this floor. Partly because they are beautiful rooms, and partly to be nearer this study."

"It seems strangely appropriate that he should die in this room," I said, glancing toward the still figure.

"It seems appropriate that he should die anywhere!" Archer muttered, in a savage undertone. And in answer to my look of surprise at this outburst, he added: "He was a brute to his wife. I'm sorry his death occurred in this horrible way, but I am not sorry he's gone."

I could make no reply; for, though I never should have put it into words, my feeling was the same. But the death had occurred in a horrible way, and the exigencies and consequences of it must be met. Doctor Mason reappeared, and in response to our inquiries, he said that Mrs. Van Wyck had regained consciousness, and was being looked after by her maid and by Mrs. Carstairs.

"I shall now telephone for the coroner," he went on. "I assume that Morland will take charge of his father's affairs; and I think that Miss Barbara should be told at once what has happened."

I couldn't help admiring the poise and practical good sense of Doctor Mason. He had been the family physician of the Van Wycks for many years, and whatever his personal feeling toward the head of the house, he now remembered only his professional responsibility and acted accordingly.

While he was telephoning the coroner, a young man came into the study, who was a stranger to me.

"Is that you, Lasseter?" said Morland, looking up. "A tragedy has occurred, and my father has been killed; by himself or another, we don't know."

Morland spoke mechanically, almost as if he felt it incumbent upon him to explain the situation. I soon discovered that Barclay Lasseter was Mr. Van Wyck's secretary. He did not live in the house, but came every morning to the study. He was the tallest man I had ever seen; of slight build, with a dark, somewhat sinister face. I couldn't help wondering if he were in any way implicated in the tragedy. Like the rest of us, he was self-possessed, and, though shocked, seemed anxious, principally, to do anything he might to help.

"Could it have been the work of burglars?" he said. "Has anything been stolen?"

"I don't know," I replied, as no one else spoke. "Do you miss anything?"

Lasseter glanced over the desk, and, taking some keys from his pocket, opened one or two drawers.

"Check-book and petty cash all right," he said briefly. "Haven't you looked in the safe?"

"No," said Morland; but he made no move to follow up Lasseter's suggestion.

I heard no sound at the doorway, but seeing Doctor Mason's eyes turn from the telephone in that direction, I looked, too, and saw Mrs. Carstairs come in.

She entered noiselessly, as she always moved, and though she was wearing the same white gown I had admired earlier that morning, she appeared altogether different. No longer was the smartness of her costume its chief characteristic. But,—and it must have been owing to the woman's wonderful dramatic ability,—her white linen garb had the effect of the uniform of a trained nurse. With a swift, comprehending glance, she looked in every one of our faces, and then, without a word glided to the chair where sat the still figure of David Van Wyck.

She betrayed no trace of self-consciousness, indeed, she seemed unaware of our presence, as she stood looking at the dead man's face. Then she spoke. "It was suicide," she said, with an air of certainty. "Mr. Van Wyck was an unhappy man, and he sought refuge in death."

For the first time, she assumed a melodramatic pose, and stood, looking at us all, as if to challenge contradiction.

"I know what you mean!" began Morland hotly; "but it is not true! My father was not an unhappy man."

Mrs. Carstairs merely gave a Frenchy shrug of her well-formed shoulders, and said nothing. With her hanging hands lightly clasped in front of her, she stood, cool and self-possessed, while Morland went on, irately.

"Since you have said that, Mrs. Carstairs, please explain yourself. Why do you say my father was unhappy?"

"I speak of what I know," she returned, her gaze at him not flinching. "But I deny your right to question me concerning my knowledge."

"If you know anything that can help to throw any light on this sad occurrence, it is your duty to tell it, Mrs. Carstairs," said Doctor Mason, speaking rather sternly.

"When I am questioned by authority, it will be time for me to speak," she returned, calmly.

Her manner and voice,—even her words,— seemed to betoken that she was in possession of great secrets, but I had an intuitive conviction that it was only pretense. I felt sure she wanted to appear sensationally important; and I wondered if she meant, in any way to make trouble for Anne.

I think the same notion was in Archer's mind, for he said:

"Any facts you may know, Mrs. Carstairs, must be told at the inquest. But opinions or fancies carry no weight."

She gave him a glance that seemed tinged with mockery, but she only said: "Mine is not a nature to exploit opinions or fancies." Then she turned to Doctor Mason, and speaking in her capacity of housekeeper, asked him concerning the removal of the body to another room.

"Not until the coroner gives permission," he replied. "He will be here shortly; and until then, we can make no changes or definite plans." Barbara came to the study door, accompanied by Mrs. Stelton and Beth Fordyce. Mrs. Carstairs moved swiftly to meet them, but though she admitted Barbara, she refused entrance to the others. I did not hear her words, as she spoke with them, but they seemed willing to accept her dictum, and turned away together. I couldn't help admiring her wisdom and tact in keeping them out, for they were emotional women, and their exclamations would have jarred the overwrought nerves of us all. Mrs. Carstairs was charming. She told Barbara in a few words, all that we knew, and clasped her arm in an unobtrusive, but helpful sympathy. But Barbara shook her off, almost rudely, and going straight to her father's side, looked at him long and silently. Then she went over and sat down by Morland and they conversed in whispers. Mrs. Carstairs was apparently not at all offended by Barbara's manner, and placidly continued her role of general director of affairs. She straightened a small rug, emptied an ash tray into a waste basket, and was about to tidy up the desk, when Condron Archer said:

"It would be wiser, Mrs. Carstairs, not to move anything, before the coroner arrives. He must see the room as it is. There may be clues to the—the intruder."

"There was no intruder," said the housekeeper, in a tone of quiet assurance. "Mr. Van Wyck died by his own hand."

But she ceased fussing among the desk appointments, and sat down near the door. She leaned her head back, and closed her eyes, looking the picture of sphinx-like inscrutability.

But she was alert enough to be at the door, as the coroner entered a moment later. She ushered him in, and seemed about to lead him toward the desk, when Doctor Mason rather peremptorily took matters in charge, himself.

The coroner, whose name was Mellen, was a brisk and somewhat aggressive man. He went at once to the body of the dead man and began his examination. He agreed with the doctor that it was difficult to tell what had caused death, except by an autopsy, but he at once began a search for the weapon. At his request, Archer and I joined him, but in the whole great room we could find no pistol nor any instrument of the nature of a stiletto.

"Then, it must be the work of an intruder," declared the coroner, "who took the weapon away with him."

"But that's impossible," I said; "for this room was absolutely secure in its locks and bolts against any intruder. Nobody could possibly have gotten in."

"But it is equally impossible that a man could have killed himself and left no trace of the weapon," said Mr. Mellen doggedly.

"Could he have stabbed or shot himself and then thrown the weapon far from him?" asked Archer, looking deeply thoughtful.

"Death was almost instantaneous," said Doctor Mason; "but I suppose that by a spasmodic muscular effort he could have done that. However, the relaxed position of his hands and arms does not make it seem probable."

"But it is the only explanation," said I eagerly. "Come on, Archer, let us make a more thorough search. Perhaps Mr. Lasseter will help us."

Barclay Lasseter agreed, though he seemed rather half-hearted about it.

Barbara and Morland looked at us, but made no offer of help.

The search was fruitless. Neither floor nor walls showed any bullet holes or powder-marks. There was no weapon to be found; though I produced the few small shot I had found on the floor, they seemed meaningless in the absence of any gun.

"The very absence of a weapon precludes all idea of suicide," said Coroner Mellen, at last; "and, though I'm not prepared to say how the murderer got in or out of this room, I believe that he did do so, and that David Van Wyck did not die by his own hand. Has anything been stolen?"

Lasseter opened the safe door, and I expressed surprise that it was unlocked.

"Often is," returned the secretary carelessly. "Most of the valuable things are in inner compartments, with complicated locks of their own. And, too, there never are burglaries in this peaceful village, and a man grows careless. But I can't see that any securities are missing. All these papers seem undisturbed."

"The pearls!" cried Morland, starting up suddenly. "Are they there?"

"Here is the box," said Lasseter, handing a jewel-case to Morland. "Open it yourself."

Morland opened it and gave a cry of despair, for the satin-lined case was empty.

"The pearls gone!" said Barbara, with an awestricken look. "Then, it was a burglar, after all."

"But it couldn't be," I began, when the coroner cut me short.

"If pearls have been stolen, of course it was a burglar," he said; "and a professional cracksman, if he could get into this room and out again."

"But he couldn't!" I declared emphatically, glancing at the windows and doors.

Still the coroner refused to heed me, and said abruptly, "What were they worth?"

"They were practically priceless," Morland stated. "My father had been collecting and matching them for years. It was a triple necklace composed of three strands of the finest and largest pearls he could procure. One hundred thousand dollars would be a conservative estimate of their value."

"And a man kept such jewels as that in an unlocked safe?" said the coroner incredulously.

"They must have been there temporarily," said Morland, as if puzzling the matter out himself.

"And, too, I've no doubt my father intended to lock the safe before he left the study. But he was murdered first."

"Have you any theory, Mr. Van Wyck, how a murder could have been effected?"

"No," said Morland; "I haven't. I know, even better than the rest of you, how absolutely this room is protected against forcible entrance. And that is one reason why my father was sometimes careless about locking the safe. He knew no one could get into this room from outside. Of course, upon leaving it at night, he always locked the door that communicates with the house, and kept the key himself."

"There is no duplicate key?" asked Mr. Mellen.

"None," said Morland positively. Then Barbara Van Wyck made a suggestion. "If Father did —did kill himself," she said hesitatingly, "possibly he himself had taken the pearls from the case and hidden them."

I realized at once what she meant. If David Van Wyck had taken his own life, it would have been quite in keeping with his cruel nature to hide the pearls where his family might not easily find them.

CHAPTER 7: THE MYSTERIOUS MOTOR CAR

"No!" cried Mrs. Carstairs, impetuously; "David Van Wyck would not do that!"

"You seem very certain," said Morland, looking at her coldly.

"I am certain," she retorted, with a flush of her dark eyes. "Do you suppose I've lived under David Van Wyck's roof all these years, without learning his nature fairly well? He was a hard man and severe,—but he was just, and above such meanness as you ascribe to him."

"But," said I, "you have already expressed an opinion that Mr. Van Wyck died by his own hand. Now, if the pearls were stolen by a burglar, it is a strange coincidence that the two crimes should occur the same night."

Mrs. Carstairs looked at me with her face full of baffled rage. Her theories were indeed at variance. If an intruder took the pearls, undoubtedly David Van Wyck had been murdered. If, on the other hand, he had committed suicide, he would seem to be himself responsible for the disappearance of the jewels.

For a moment Mrs. Carstairs sat motionless, though it was evident her mind was working rapidly. The rest of us sat watching her, and I, at any rate, began to feel a dawning hope that what she might say next would throw a little light on the mystery.

At last she burst out, in a voice low, but tense with feeling: "I am sure David Van Wyck killed himself. I am sure that if before his death he secreted that valuable pearl necklace, he was entirely justified in doing so."

"Just what do you mean by that?" demanded Archer, angrily.

"I think you all know, without being told," returned Mrs. Carstairs, and her lips curled unpleasantly.

"Nevertheless, you shall tell!" and Archer's voice fairly quivered with indignation. "Speak out before us all, and say what you mean by your insinuation."

Mrs. Carstairs looked at him with an air half supercilious and half amused.

"Who are you, Mr. Archer," she said, "that you should arraign me, in this manner?"

"And who are you," thundered Archer, "that you should presume to cast aspersions at any of the Van Wyck family?"

Mr. Mellen broke in upon this controversy.

"What position do you hold in this house, Mrs. Carstairs?" he inquired, in a tone of such authority that it compelled a respectful answer.

"I have been Mr. Van Wyck's housekeeper for seven years."

"You were here, then, before he was married to the present Mrs. Van Wyck?"

"Five years before."

The very tones of the housekeeper's voice, the reminiscent look in her beautiful mysterious eyes, and the almost insolent toss of her well-poised head, fully confirmed my previous thought that she had deeply resented the advent of Anne.

Coroner Mellen looked at her a moment, and then said, as if dismissing her, "You will, of course, be called upon to give your testimony at the inquest."

His curt nod of dismissal was sufficient to send Mrs. Carstairs from the room, but she paid no heed to it, and remained sitting in her chair, without a trace of embarrassment or self-consciousness. I couldn't help admiring her aplomb,—her wonderful self-poise; nor could I help wondering whether she knew anything about the tragedy, or whether her sensational nature made her wish to appear mysterious.

I began to like the coroner. He was not prepossessing in appearance, being extremely young for his position, and of a sandy-haired, freckle-faced type that made him look like a blushing school-boy. But his blue eyes showed a quick intelligence, and I jumped to the conclusion that he was bright and intuitive, but inexperienced.

"I must ask a few preliminary questions," he said, and there was a little nervous hesitation in his manner, "and I will hold my inquest this afternoon. Doctor Mason, can you tell me at what time the death of Mr. Van Wyck probably occurred?"

"He has been dead, fully nine or ten hours," replied the doctor; "it is probable that he was killed about or after midnight. I refuse to accept the theory of suicide."

"Was death instantaneous?" went on Mr. Mellen.

"It was; though I shall make further examination, I am already convinced that Mr. Van Wyck was stabbed with a sharp weapon by some one with murderous intent."

"But nobody could get in!" exclaimed Mrs. Carstairs, and she sat forward, grasping the arms of her chair and gazing intently at the doctor, as if she would hypnotize him.

Although I had begun to dislike the woman, I was forced to admit to myself her marvellous charm. Every pose she assumed seemed more graceful, more picturesque than the one before; and yet I couldn't help thinking that her effects were all carefully premeditated. She showed no self-consciousness, but her self-reliance and self-sufficiency were so marked, that I believed her a consummate actress.

"We are not considering that now," said Mr. Mellen, looking at her keenly, and then turning to Morland, he said, "Who discovered your father's body?"

Morland told briefly the circumstances of breaking in the door, and the coroner listened attentively and thoughtfully.

"Summon the valet," he said, abruptly. Mrs. Carstairs rose with a sudden start and exclaimed, "Why do you want him? He is in no way implicated in this matter! He did not attend his master last evening."

"Good Heavens, madam," said the coroner, amazed at this outbreak, "nobody has accused him! Pray, calm yourself. Why do you object to his presence here?"

"He is my son," said Mrs. Carstairs.

"And if he is, that is no reason he should not be questioned." Mr. Mellen gave a grim smile, and shook his head slightly, as if to imply that Mrs. Carstairs was a woman beyond his ken.

Morland had touched a bell, in response to which the valet appeared. He had little to tell, save to corroborate Morland's story of the morning; but had he, himself, been guilty of crime he could not have acted more frightened. I remembered, however, that he had shown the same behavior when the alarm was first raised, and I concluded that it was merely a natural horror of death; and perhaps he had inherited his mother's emotional disposition. But whatever Mrs. Carstairs's attitude toward David Van Wyck or his family, I now perceived that the woman's all-absorbing passion was her son. She watched him with intensity. Her mobile face unconsciously followed the expressions of his countenance. She prompted his speech when he hesitated; and she interrupted, and spoke for him so frequently that Mr. Mellen was obliged to reprimand her.

But between the trembling valet and his anxious and apprehensive mother, nothing was learned that seemed to be of the least importance. It seemed, that as Mr. Van Wyck expected to be up late with the committeemen, he had excused Carstairs from attending him when he retired, and the valet had had the evening to himself. When he went to his Master's bedroom that morning, he found it had been unoccupied through the night, and he had raised an alarm. The rest of his story was exactly the same as Morland's.

I could not see why his mother should be so wrought up over the matter of his appearance, but I set it down to an excessive maternal solicitude, lest he should be suspected of implication in the tragedy.

"This committee," went on Mr. Mellen, his brows bent in perplexity, "who were they?"

"Three gentlemen from the village," said Morland. "They met with my father last night, to discuss a business matter. They all went away before I left this room."

Suddenly Lasseter made an announcement. He had been looking over the papers that lay on the desk, and he said abruptly, "The deed of gift is gone."

"What do you mean?" asked Coroner Mellen, alert for further information.

"Last night," said Lasseter, "I was here during the conference of the gentlemen from the village and Mr. Van Wyck. He made out to them a deed of gift of a large sum of money. However, he retained this paper after his visitors had left. He may have put it away after I left, myself, but so far I cannot find it."

"At what time did you leave?" asked the coroner.

"Almost exactly at midnight," returned the secretary.

"And where was the deed you speak of then?"

"Lying on this desk, in front of Mr. Van Wyck."

"Who was here when you left, besides Mr. Van Wyck?"

"Only his son, Morland."

"That's a lie!" exclaimed Morland, springing up. "When I left this room at midnight, you were here alone with my father!"

To my surprise, the coroner did not question these contradictory statements. He looked at the two men without speaking, though his sharp blue eyes showed that he had understood what they said.

"The case is most mysterious," he declared; "and I think it wiser to have no further discussion or investigation until I can hold the inquest and hear definite testimony. The facts of the absolutely inaccessible room and the entire absence of the fatal weapon are so irreconcilable, that I confess I am baffled. I think the only course to pursue, is to engage the services of a clever and experienced detective."

"There is no occasion for such a thing," said Mrs. Carstairs, quite as if she were in authority; "I object to it very decidedly."

The coroner looked at her appraisingly, and then turned to Morland Van Wyck. Though he said no word, it was quite evident he was inquiring from whom he should take orders. My liking for Mr. Mellen deepened. He showed brains and commonsense, two qualities not always found together, and not universally the attributes of coroners.

"Your opinion is not wanted, Mrs. Carstairs," Morland said pettishly, but I noticed he did not look at her. "I, too, think we should have a detective. What do you say, Barbara?"

Miss Van Wyck hesitated. "I hate the publicity of it," she said; "but I think we ought to find the pearls."

I looked at her in surprise. Were her thoughts all for the jewels, and had she no desire to find and bring to justice the murderer of her father? Then I remembered that her theory was, that David Van Wyck had secreted the pearls and then killed himself.

"Not only the pearls," Morland was saying; "we must lay bare the whole mystery. I cannot live, not knowing how my father met his death. If some villain killed him, the murderer must be brought to justice."

Morland strode up and down the room as he talked, and I thought I had never seen him look more manly. I felt a new respect for him, and a willingness to help him in any way I might.

"Of course," Morland went on, "we must not make definite arrangements without consulting my Mrs. Van Wyck. It is for her to say whether we shall engage a detective." He flashed a defiant glance at Mrs. Carstairs, as he spoke, but it did not ruffle the calm of that self-reliant personage.

Barbara went away to confer with Anne on the subject, and soon returned saying that her stepmother expressed entire indifference in the matter. She was perfectly willing that the detective should be engaged, if Barbara and Morland wished it.

"Do you know of a good detective, Mr. Mellen?" I asked, while my thoughts flew to Fleming Stone and his marvellous ability. But that great detective was far away, and so, unavailable.

"I know of none in Crescent Falls Village," returned the coroner, "but I can send for a very good man from the city. His name is Markham, and I have reason to know he is exceedingly clever and successful; and though not a low-priced man, his fees are not exorbitant."

"Thank you, Mr. Mellen," said Barbara, simply; "that is the kind of man I should like to investigate this case. I am sure I am correct in my beliefs, and I think a detective can find the pearls for us. There is no other crime to be discovered."

"That is what I think!" And moved by a sympathy of opinions, Mrs. Carstairs glided up to Barbara and took her hands. But she found herself coldly repulsed, as Miss Van Wyck said curtly, "Do you?" And drawing her hands from the clasp of the housekeeper, she moved slowly toward the door, with a backward glance at the still figure of her father.

And then came the undertaker and his men, and the coroner dismissed all of us, except Doctor Mason. As we all walked silently through the corridor, Morland and Barbara turned aside into Anne's room. I asked them to assure Mrs. Van Wyck of my sympathy, and to tell her how glad I would be if I might do anything for her. The message sounded perfunctory, but I think I had never said sincerer words.

The rest of us went various ways, Archer going off to his own room, and Mrs. Carstairs toward the servants' wing.

I went to the library, and after a short time, Morland joined me there.

"How is Mrs. Van Wyck?" I inquired.

"She's composed," he answered briefly; "but exhausted from the shock. She is entirely unable to discuss details of arrangements, and says for Barbara and myself to manage things as we choose. She sends thanks for your kind message, and hopes to see you later in the day."

My heart gave a throb at this, for though I was longing to see Anne, I wanted the suggestion to come from her.

"Then of course you will take complete authority," I said to Morland, who sat on the edge of a table, moodily swinging one foot back and forth.

"Yes," he said angrily, "if I can circumvent that Carstairs woman."

I had resolved to be very discreet on this subject, so I only said, "She is a strange personality."

"She's a serpent!" Morland muttered, and just then Mrs. Stelton and Miss Fordyce appeared at the doorway.

"Mayn't we come in?" begged Mrs. Stelton, in her pouting, childish way; "we're so frightened and lonesome!"

Beth Fordyce said nothing, but her big blue eyes were full of tears, as she looked at Morland.

"Certainly," I said, rising; "please come in and talk to me."

The latter speech seemed necessary, for at their entrance, Morland walked out of the room without a word.

"Poor Mr. Morland," said Mrs. Stelton, wringing her little hands, fussily; "I am so sorry for him! I wish I could comfort him."

"I think he likes best to be let alone," I said; "aside from his natural sorrow, he is suddenly loaded with grave responsibilities; enough to overwhelm any man."

"They will not overwhelm him." It was Miss Fordyce who spoke, and her eyes had the far-away look that always showed in them when her mood was occult. "*I* shall care for his spirit, and sustain him in his hour "

"Now, Beth, let up on that rubbish!" And Mrs. Stelton was so in earnest, that she forgot to flutter.

"You tell Mr. Sturgis what you have to tell him."

"I've nothing to tell," and Miss Fordyce looked positively dreamy.

"Yes, you have!" and Mrs. Stelton took her arm and shook her slightly. "Wake up, now, and stop your nonsense! Tell Mr. Sturgis what you saw last night."

"Was it a vision?" I asked, resigning myself to one of her usual psychic experiences.

"I did have a vision--" the girl began, but Mrs. Stelton interrupted her again.

"Never mind your vision,—stick to plain facts! You tell Mr. Sturgis the story, just exactly as you told it to me!"

"What is it?" I asked, interested now, and hoping it might be something of real importance.

"Please tell me at once, Miss Fordyce, for some one may come in here at any moment."

As she frequently did, Miss Fordyce changed her manner suddenly, and spoke with alert energy.

"It's only this. I was wakeful last night, and I rose and sat by my window for a long time. The moon was bright, and everything looked so beautiful, it did my soul good. Well, as I sat there--"

"Excuse me a moment, Miss Fordyce, which is your room?"

"Directly over this," she replied; "on the second floor."

"I have the front room on the other side of the second floor," I said, realizing that she could not see the East wing from her window.

"Yes, I know," said Mrs. Stelton; "you have the room directly over Anne's. Mr. Archer's room is over Mr. Van Wyck's bedroom. Mr. Van Wyck used to have the room Mr. Archer has now, before he married Anne. Then he had the first floor suite done up, and positively the rooms are of regal splendor. Why, Anne's dressing-room--"

"Go on with your story, please, Miss Fordyce," I said, taking advantage of one of Mrs. Stelton's pauses for breath.

"As I sat by my window," the girl went on, "I saw a very large motor car come slowly along the main road. It halted now and then, not as if because of any mechanical trouble, but as if its driver hesitated about proceeding. After stopping two or three times, it finally came into the grounds, and up our main road. But it continued to pause now and then until at last it made a mad dash around the house, passing right under my window. I didn't see the car again, but a few moments later, I saw some person wrapped in a large coat, walk stealthily by my window. I don't know whether it was a man or a woman, but whoever it was, seemed afraid of being seen. For the dark figure hid twice behind trees, and then suddenly ran swiftly away in the same direction the motor car had gone."

"At what time did all this happen?" I asked.

"I'm not sure; but it was not far from midnight. At any rate, between twelve and one."

"Miss Fordyce," I said, "as you know, a great mystery at present surrounds the death of Mr. Van Wyck. This incident you saw, may have a bearing on the matter, and it may not. But won't you promise me not to speak of it to anyone else? And at the coroner's inquest, which will be held this afternoon, won't you tell this story simply and straightforwardly, as you have told it to me?"

"At the inquest!" Miss Fordyce exclaimed; "oh, I just couldn't!"

"Yes, you can!" I answered her, sternly, "and you must. If you do it rightly, you may be of great help to the whole Van Wyck family; while, if you are foolish about it, you may impede justice and cause untold trouble."

"There, I told you so!" cried Mrs. Stelton. "I knew it was important. Now, Beth, you come along with me. I'll see to it, Mr. Sturgis, that this girl tells her story and tells it right, when she is called upon to do so."

"Thank you, Mrs. Stelton," I said, heartily, and I had never liked the little lady so well before. "Keep Miss Fordyce up to the mark and don't let her slip away into her dreams and visions." The two went away together, and I started off for a stroll by myself, to see what a little fresh air would do towards straightening out the complex questions that were baffling my brain.

CHAPTER 8: ENTER A DETECTIVE

I WALKED along the paths, my eyes cast down, and my hands behind me, while I brooded over the situation. I had the grace to be utterly ashamed of the fact, that beneath all other considerations, I was conscious of a realization that Anne was now free. I would not allow myself to put this thought into words; I tried to evade and ignore it; but it brought a peace to my soul that shone steadily through all the disturbing problems that filled my consciousness.

First, was the great problem of Van Wyck's death. Was it suicide or murder? And then I thought, how futile even to wonder about that, until the inquest, when unexpected disclosures might immediately solve the mystery.

Next was the problem of what Anne would do. But that, it seemed to me, was an indelicacy even to think about, at present. So I resolutely put it away from me, and turned my thoughts to the story Beth Fordyce had told. It was certainly strange that a motor should come into the Van Wyck estate at midnight, and that it should alternately halt and proceed in such a mysterious manner. Also that its entrance and disappearance should be followed by the presence of a stealthy, cloaked figure.

But again, was Beth Fordyce's word reliable? I had no doubt of her integrity;—but the girl had such strange fancies and such a vivid imagination, that I could not place implicit reliance on the story as she had told it.

To her distorted mental vision, a belated pedestrian might assume the mystery of a prowling marauder. And yet, she had said the figure passed under her window, which would of course mean some one intending, either rightly or wrongfully, to enter the house. And, too, the strange proceedings of the motor car,—though perhaps exaggerated by her,— could scarcely be all imagination, unless the girl had wilfully made up this story, which I did not believe. But again, if the occupant of the motor car had indeed been a criminal,—a thief and a murderer,— with fell intent against David Van Wyck, how had he entered the study, committed his crimes, and departed again, leaving every outlet of the room securely fastened on the inside?

This question proved unanswerable, so I gave it up and began to retrace my steps toward the house. As I neared the stables, I noticed a man coming along the same road that I had seen Mrs. Carstairs slowly following, early that same morning. I paused a moment to watch him, and I saw that it was Carstairs, the valet. To my surprise, he repeated exactly the procedure of his mother. He stepped along slowly, carefully examining the ground, and had every appearance of a man searching for some small, lost article. He had a stick in his hand, and he even scraped the dirt of the road now and then, peering closely, as if in a desperate search.

I determined to come upon him suddenly, as I had surprised his mother, and see if he were as apt at explaining himself as she had been.

I approached very quietly, and as I was just at his elbow, I said, "What have you lost?"

The man dropped his stick, and raised a white, startled face.

"N-nothing,—sir. I assure you,—I have lost nothing!"

"What are you looking for, then? I will help you find it!"

I picked up the stick he had dropped, and began poking in the dust, myself. But he said, stammering, and with a pleading expression:

"N-no! I have not lost anything, sir. Give me back my stick, I beg of you."

"Look here, Carstairs, it's no crime to lose anything. But to be so secret about it, and so rattled, betokens a guilty conscience of some sort."

"Yes, sir; very good, sir. I'm not rattled, sir,— and indeed, indeed, sir, I have not lost anything."

Clearly the man had not his mother's faculty for rising to a situation. Without a doubt they had both been searching for the same thing, as I saw them both closely examining the ground in the same place. But she had tossed off my questions with witty repartee, while he was the embodiment of agonized embarrassment.

I went on toward the house, with a new problem added to my brain collection,—the problem of the two searchers, who both denied having lost anything, and who were mother and son. Collusion and secrecy were certainly shown here. I had no clue to the solution of this mystery, and thought that very likely it was a matter of no importance, anyway. When I reached the house, Barbara met me with the welcome news that Anne desired to see me. I was conducted to her dressing-room, and as I entered, I realized the truth of what I had been told regarding the Van Wycks' apartments. A more exquisite gem of a room, I never saw. It was furnished entirely in Louis Seize effects and was a miracle of gilded carving and rose-colored brocade.

"And you call this a dressing-room!" I said, endeavoring to be casual; "I think boudoir a more appropriate term."

Anne smiled. "I hate a French word," she said, "when English will do as well. And I especially dislike the term 'sitting-room,' so what could I do? And it is my dressing-room, as you see." She waved her hand toward a daintily appointed toilet-table, glittering with glass and gold.

I scarcely knew whether to continue the conversation on trivial matters, or whether to speak of the tragedy. Anne herself was perfectly composed; though pale, and with an air of forcing herself to be quiet and natural. But after a few moments of beating time, I said, "Let's not evade the subject that fills both our minds. May we not speak of it?"

"How nice you are!" said Anne, and her eyes beamed with gratitude. "You always do the right thing, Raymond. My heart is bursting to talk of these things, yet everyone thinks I don't want to!"

"Talk to me," I said, gently, "just as you will. Say anything that is in your heart."

I was on dangerous ground, and I knew it, but I held myself well in hand. Anne looked lovelier than ever, in a white lacy sort of boudoir gown and a lace cap on her beautiful hair. Also she looked pathetic and as if greatly in need of some one to lean on for sympathy and counsel.

"Let us talk it over freely," I said; "you cannot be brave and courageous, Anne, as you must be, if you are afraid to face the facts. You don't think your husband took his own life, do you?"

"I'm sure he did not. David had no reason for such an act. He was a man fond of life; and beside, he had this project of the library in mind, and he was more than anxious to carry it through. There is no reason,—there can be no reason,—why he should kill himself. But Raymond," and her white brows drew tensely, "how could anyone kill him and get away afterward, leaving the study locked? I've thought over that until I'm nearly crazy. You see *I* know how perfectly impossible it is to get into that room when the door is locked. Because—"

"Because what?" I gently prompted her.

A look of pain came into her eyes, followed by a sudden determination; and she went on: "I may as well tell you; because my husband and I have had some fearful quarrels. Invariably he would go and shut himself in the study afterward. I knew it was my duty to try to make peace with him and often I have tried to get into the study in spite of him. I have even tried to get in at a window, while he would sit inside and smile at me in mockery."

"What you have been through with that man!" I exclaimed.

"Yes; and yet he was often very good to me. At times he was a perfect brute, but it was because of his really ungovernable temper. Then again he would fairly spoil me with kindness. But of late his kindness had become more and more rare, and he was sarcastic and cruel much of the time. I tell you this, Raymond, because I want you to understand, that while I respected and admired David in many ways, I cannot mourn him as I would mourn a man I loved."

This admission brought joy to my own heart, but I knew this was no time or place to let it be known, and as a matter of precaution, I hurriedly changed the subject.

"What a strange woman Mrs. Carstairs is," I said; "had she an especial interest in Mr. Van Wyck?"

"Oh, she adored him," and Anne spoke carelessly as if it were a matter of no moment to her. "At one time she hoped to marry him, but David had no such intention. So of course she resented my presence here, and has never been nice to me. It didn't bother me much, though she is annoying. I tried to have her dismissed, but Carstairs is such a perfect valet, David would not give him up, so they both remained. Now they can both go!"

Anne spoke with a sudden vindictiveness, and just at that moment Mrs. Carstairs appeared in the open doorway. Her arrival was so opportune that I felt positive she had been listening outside the door.

She did not seem angry, but there was a feline note in her voice as she said, "You were speaking of me, Mrs. Van Wyck?"

It is a tribute to Anne's wonderful poise that she was in no way ruffled. She spoke quietly, as she replied, "Yes, Mrs. Carstairs, since you chanced to overhear, I am quite willing to repeat what I said. As there is no longer any occasion for your son's services, you will doubtless prefer to go away with him. But I beg you will consult your own

pleasure as to the time of your departure, and not feel
obliged to make inconvenient haste."

It was a clash of superior forces. If Anne showed self-
control, the housekeeper was even more absolutely at
ease.

"Thank you, Mrs. Van Wyck," she returned, in silvery
tones; "I shall take advantage of your kind permission,
and remain here, at least until we have discovered the
solution of the mystery that surrounds the death of Mr.
Van Wyck. It may be that I can be of assistance to you."

"I scarcely think that," and Anne's slight smile would
have rasped a saint; "but you are at liberty to stay as long
as you choose."

The latter part of the speech was almost patronizing,
and distinctly in the manner of a mistress to a servant,
and it scored. Mrs. Carstairs's eyes flashed, and she
winced as if flicked with a whip; but in an instant she had
dropped her eyelids, and though she merely said " Thank
you," and left the room, her air was so unvanquished,
even victorious, that she really had the final word.

"You see," said Anne, spreading her hands,
deprecatingly, "one cannot contend with that sort of
thing, except between equals!"

"I appreciate that perfectly," I returned, very
seriously; "but you must realize, Anne, that she is a
dangerous woman. You are no match for her; because,
though you have marvellous perceptions and mental
powers, yet you are innocent and rightminded. That
woman is all wrong. I don't know in what respects,—I
don't know anything about her. But she is capable of
crime!"

To my consternation, Anne turned white to the very
lips. She put her hands before her eyes as if to shut out
some dreadful sight, and she moaned in a whisper, "Oh,
Raymond, I am capable of crime, too!"

"There, there," I said, soothingly, "that woman has
wrought on your nerves. For that matter, child,

everybody is capable of crime. I had no business to say what I did. I'm a churl,—a mischief-maker."

Anne lifted her eyes and almost smiled at my selfabasement, and then, as her maid entered the room, she said, "What is it, Jeannette?"

"Mr. Archer, madame. He wishes to see you."

"Tell him to come in," said Anne, graciously, and then herself added, "Come on in, Connie. There's no one here but Mr. Sturgis."

Archer came in, looking preoccupied. With scant ceremony he threw himself into a chair, and said abruptly: "Now, look here, Anne, how about this detective? Do you want him to come?"

"No," said Anne, simply.

"I thought so. Now Mellen has sent for him, and unless we telephone contrary orders or something, he'll be here to-day."

"Why don't you want him, Anne?" I asked, in astonishment. "I think it is necessary to have him. The mystery must be cleared up, and, too the missing pearls must be found. Surely a detective could help."

"Well, then, let him come!" Anne spoke almost pettishly, and I suddenly realized that her composure was forced, and her self-control was beginning to give way.

"I think," said Archer to me, "that Mrs. Van Wyck's wishes should be law in this matter."

"Of course," I agreed, "but perhaps Mrs. Van Wyck doesn't realize how customary it is, and how necessary it is to employ a detective in such a case as this."

"I needn't see him, need I?" asked Anne, raising imploring eyes to mine.

"No," I began, when Archer interrupted: "Of course you'll have to see him, and he'll ask you all sorts of questions, and tangle you up so that you won't know what you're saying."

As usual, Anne did the unexpected. She suddenly assumed a dignified, even haughty air, and said: "Let him come. Let him question me as much as he likes. I'm not afraid of such questioning! When will he arrive?"

"I don't know," said Archer, "probably this afternoon, or perhaps before luncheon. I'm glad you're getting your nerve back, Anne, for the inquest will be held this afternoon, and you will have to testify. Now don't let yourself get rattled."

"I shall not get rattled," Anne said, slowly.

"But, Connie, I don't want to testify, or whatever you call it. Why should I? I don't know who killed David, or anything about it."

"But you will be called on," said Archer, "and you must keep your head. Don't break down or anything. Answer the questions directly and shortly, and you'll soon be let off."

This was good, sound advice, and I was glad Archer gave it to her. I wished she would look to me more for counsel or help, but she seemed to depend on Archer, as on an old friend. Indeed, after a time, she said, "Run away now, will you, Raymond; I have some things I want to talk over with Connie alone."

This summary dismissal nearly took my breath away, but I rose and went off nonchalantly, hiding my chagrin as best I could.

Immediately after luncheon the detective came. Mr. Markham was a commonplace-looking man, of a manner somewhat self-assured. He was perhaps even a trifle conceited, but he seemed to have commonsense and a good grasp of the logical. He was quick and alert of manner and went about his work in a systematic and methodical way. The household was divided as to the necessity for his presence. Morland and Barbara seemed to want him, but Anne and Archer refused to see him unless absolutely necessary.

For some reason, Barclay Lasseter appeared deeply incensed at his presence. Indeed, the secretary abruptly took his hat and went home when Mr. Markham arrived, saying he would return for the inquest.

For myself, I listened eagerly to the detective's opinions. Of course, he was allowed immediate access to the study, and of course, he made a careful examination of the whole room. But he found nothing that would throw any light on the mystery, and I felt a little disappointed at his non-committal attitude. He spent much time examining locks and bolts and inquiring as to keys. But he only proved, what we had known before, that the study was absolutely inaccessible to an intruder. Then, of course, he declared it must have been a suicide. Then, when he was convinced of the utter absence of any weapon, and the practical impossibility of the wound being self-inflicted, he returned to the theory of murder.

He was greatly enthused over the mystery of the case and the contradictory evidence.

"If I may say so," he observed, pompously, "I have been especially fortunate and successful in the criminal cases which I have undertaken. I have the instinct of a sleuth, and I discover clues where none seems to exist. But I never before have had the kind of a case that depends upon proving the presence of an intruder in a locked room. Now, we know that no one could have entered this room and left it, locked as it was. And yet, if not a case of suicide, some one did do so. It is for me to discover how."

Mr. Markham made this speech with such an air of having made a discovery, that I was not surprised when Morland said, brusquely:

"We knew already, Mr. Markham, that my father's death was either a suicide or a murder. We knew, too, that this room was so securely barred and bolted that we had to force an entrance. Now we have sent for you to learn if possible the truth of the matter. But what we want, is not the propounding of the problem, but its solution."

Mr. Markham did not appear at all offended by this, and only said, "Quite so, quite so, Mr. Van Wyck. Now I must remind you that aside from the crime of murder, we have the loss of the pearls to consider. I must not only solve the mystery of your father's death, but I must recover those valuable gems. Very well. I am not, of course, able to do these things in a moment, but by careful investigation and some shrewd deduction, I hope to succeed, in time."

"Of course, Mr. Markham," said Morland, "I didn't expect results at once. Pursue your own methods and call on any of us for such information or help as you may desire. Pray consider the house at your disposal, interview the servants if you choose, and feel at liberty to do what you will, unquestioned."

"I shall also," returned the detective, "expect to be allowed to interview members of the family or guests."

"That, of course," said Morland; "but I must ask of you to spare the feelings of the family as far as you possibly can, and to intrude upon the guests as little as may be."

I was not surprised at this from Morland, for it seemed to me that the detective was of a nature so zealous and so unheedful of others' feelings, that he might easily prove an annoying interviewer.

CHAPTER 9: THE INQUEST

LUNCHEON was served informally. The members of the household and the guests drifted in and out of the dining-room, where the footmen served them from a buffet. It chanced that I sat down with Morland and Archer.

We all said little, but though Morland was quiet, it seemed as though we were endeavoring not to talk, though he really wanted to.

"Would you rather we went away?" Archer asked of him; "perhaps you would prefer not to have any guests at present."

"No, no," said Morland a little irritably. "You two fellows stay on, of course. Perhaps you can help me, and Lord knows I need help. As to the ladies, they must do as they choose. Mrs. Stelton wants to remain; but I fear these awful scenes will prove too much for the nerves of Miss Fordyce. She is so highly strung "

"These scenes are enough to shake the nerves of anybody," I put in; "and you know, Morland, without being told, that Archer and I stand ready to help you in any way we can. But I confess I can't find anything to do by way of assistance."

"Nor I," said Archer, "but if our presence here makes it any easier for you, here we stay as long as you wish. At any rate we can meet some of the visitors, and save you or Mrs. Van Wyck that annoyance."

Of course everyone in the village knew of the tragedy by this time, and flocks of curious people were gathering in and about the house. Soon the whole place was in a turmoil. Neighbors and village people were coming and going, and everybody was making suggestions or proppunding theories.

Barbara and Morland quarrelled openly; Anne refused to see anybody; Archer stood around, moody and taciturn; the languid figure of Beth Fordyce could be seen strolling about the gardens, wringing her hands in picturesque despair; while Mrs. Stelton fluttered about everywhere, asking absurd questions and making herself a general nuisance.

I longed for a little talk with Anne, but decided not to bother her, so I employed myself answering the questions of the curious visitors who came and went.

The whole village was up in arms. And yet nobody seemed to care very much that David Van Wyck was dead. Their all-absorbing interest was the mystery of the thing. They positively gloated over the seemingly contradictory facts that a man had met his death in an inaccessible room and yet apparently not by his own hand.

Dozens of explanations were offered, some ingenious, some ridiculous; but I listened to them all, hoping that perhaps a chance shot might hit the truth. For I too was deeply interested in solving the mystery. Quite apart from my personal connection with the matter, I felt a stirring of the detective instinct to solve the problem. And not the least curious phase of it was that apparently nobody accused or even suspected any individual. The whole argument seemed to be that it must have been the work of an expert burglar, and yet that the entrance of such an intruder was impossible!

Buttonwood Terrace, hitherto so exclusive, was thrown open to all. Beside the curiosity seekers from the village, many personal friends and some distant relatives arrived at the house.

As both Anne and Barbara declined to see anybody, Mrs. Carstairs acted as hostess. She was serene and composed, but with an air of calm determination that made me wonder what her thoughts might be. At one time I saw her in earnest colloquy with Mr. Markham. I burned to know what she was talking about and I asked him.

"Oh," he said, "she doesn't want to testify at the inquest, and she doesn't want her son to, either. But of course they'll have to."

"Can he or they be implicated?" I asked, with interest.

"Probably not. More likely it's a woman's natural instinct to dread such an experience both for herself and for anyone dear to her."

I thought then of the peculiar circumstances of Carstairs and his mother both hunting for something in the road, and both denying that they had lost anything. I was about to tell this to Mr. Markham when he was called away on some matter. And I thought too, perhaps it was better not to mention the subject until I should discover what developments might result from the inquest.

Coroner Mellen proved himself capable of conducting matters in a business-like way. If he appeared hard and heartless it was probably necessary, considering the work he had to do. The inquest was to be held at half-past two, and there was much to be done by way of preparation. The jurymen were arriving, also several policemen and a number of reporters.

The incoming trains brought people from the city, and many of the principal men of the village were in attendance. Not everyone was allowed to enter the house, but the grounds were thronged with curiosity-seekers and idlers.

As the time neared for the inquest, the great hall began to be filled with people. A table had been placed in the centre for the use of the coroner and the reporters, and a group of chairs near by were intended for the jury.

Seats were reserved for the members of the household, and the rest of the room was quickly filled by an interested if horrified audience.

The coroner and the jurymen filed in and took their places, and as if by the touch of a magic wand, the

beautiful reception hall was transformed into a court-
room.

The arrival of the family upon the scene created a
decided stir amongst the audience.

Anne came first, walking with Condron Archer. Her
beautiful face was white, but her eyes were not cast
down; instead, she looked straight ahead of her, but with
an unseeing gaze, as if walking in sleep. Archer led her to
a chair and sat down beside her. They were followed
immediately by Barbara and Morland, who were
whispering together as they came in. This brother and
sister were often at variance in their opinions and
apparently the present occasion offered them opportunity
for differing views.

Mrs. Stelton and Miss Fordyce followed them, both
looking very much disturbed and embarrassed.

I, myself, came in with Markham, the detective, and
behind us were Mrs. Carstairs and her son. The other
servants were congregated in a nearby room, but Mrs.
Carstairs had insisted on having her son by her side and
it had been allowed.

Coroner Mellen was short and sharp in his speech,
and wasted little time in preliminaries. His jury was
sworn, and his first witness on the stand, almost before I
realized that the inquest had begun.

The valet, Carstairs, was the first one questioned. He
answered the coroner in a nervous and agitated manner,
and it was clear to be seen that he was exceedingly ill at
ease. To me, however, this was only a natural result of
finding himself implicated in such a tragedy.

"Tell the story in your own way," said Coroner Mellen,
speaking a little more kindly, as he observed the man's
demeanor.

"I went to the master's room this morning, sir, as I
always do, and he wasn't there, and his bed hadn't been
slept in. So as I couldn't think of any place he might be,
except in his study, I went there, sir, and it was locked,
and I couldn't get in. I knocked several times, but nobody

answered; so I went and told Jeannette, and she told Mrs. Van Wyck."

"Who is Jeannette?" asked Mr. Mellen.

"She's Mrs. Van Wyck's maid, sir. And then the gentlemen came from the dining-room, and they ordered the door broken in, sir. We called Ranney for that."

"Never mind about that now; tell us of last evening. When did you see Mr. Van Wyck last?"

"When he was dressing for dinner, sir. And he told me then that I needn't attend him when he retired. He said he expected some visitors in the evening, and as he should be up late I needn't wait up for him."

"And didn't you?"

"N-no, sir."

"Why did you hesitate at that reply?"

"I—I didn't, sir."

"You did. What time did you go to bed yourself last night?"

"At—at about midnight, sir."

"And where were you all the evening?"

"I was down in the village. I went to a ball there."

"And returned home about midnight?"

"Why—yes, sir."

The valet did seem disingenuous, and I felt sure that the coroner doubted his truthfulness. But to my mind the man was merely confused by the questions shot at him.

During the examination Mrs. Carstairs sat looking at her son. Her hands were clasped in the intensity of her attention, and I could see that she was controlling her agitation by sheer force of will. I had no reason to think the valet had killed his master, but I couldn't help surmising that either he or his mother, or both, knew something of the mystery that the others did not. I saw the coroner was about to dismiss the witness, and I scribbled a hasty line and passed it to Mr. Mellen, advising him to ask the valet further questions about the evening before.

The coroner seemed a little at sea in the matter, but he followed my advice.

"Did you see any of the members of the household on your return last night?"

"N-no—sir."

Either the man was actually scared out of his wits, or he was concealing something; for a more stammering, frightened witness I never saw.

"Are you sure of this?"

An affirmative nod was the only answer, and the valet's fingers laced and interlaced until I feared he would injure them.

"The servants,—did you see any of them?"

"Why—yes, sir," and Carstairs's eyes rolled wildly, as though he had made a terrifying admission.

"Which ones?"

"Only Jeannette, sir."

"Where did you see her?"

"In the servants' dining-room, sir."

"What was she doing there, at midnight?"

"She was just about to go to attend on Mrs. Van Wyck, sir."

I saw Jeannette's white face peeping in from the next room, and she looked about as terrified as the valet himself. In an undertone, I drew Mr. Markham's attention to this fact, but he seemed to think it unimportant, and said that servants were always rattled at being made publicly conspicuous. I didn't entirely agree with him, and I felt fully convinced that Carstairs and Jeannette had knowledge of some sort bearing on the tragedy. I glanced at Anne, and found that she, like Mrs. Carstairs, was simply holding herself together by strong will power.

The others were not so deeply affected. The Van Wyck brother and sister were quiet and composed, though Morland had that same effect of being ready to break out indignantly at any moment. Mrs. Stelton was frankly interested in the proceedings, and showed it in her eager countenance; but Miss Fordyce sat with closed eyes, as if overcome by the whole affair. Archer looked grave, but as he continually glanced toward Anne, I was certain that he felt even more solicitude for her well-being than for the developments of the case.

Apparently the coroner thought the valet's evidence not of crucial importance, for he concluded by saying:

"Did you see any of the members of the household on your return?"

"None but the servants, sir."

"You didn't see Mr. Van Wyck in his room or in his study?"

"No, sir; I did not."

This answer, at least, was given without hesitation, and, apparently satisfied, the coroner dismissed the witness.

Ranney, the garage mechanician, was next called. His testimony was straightforward, and he was entirely unembarrassed, and indeed seemed almost uninterested.

"Mr. Morland called me," he said, "and ordered me to pick the lock of the study door. Of course, with my knowledge of mechanics, I could do this; and as it was then bolted, he ordered me to saw out the piece of wood containing the bolt. This I did, and we opened the door."

"You live in the house?" asked Mr. Mellen.

"No, sir; I live in a cottage near the stables and garage."

"What time did you retire last night?"

"Early, sir; between nine and ten o'clock."

"Were you awake at or about midnight?"

Before replying, Ranney gave a long steady glance at Carstairs. The valet returned it with a belligerent stare that seemed to convey a threat. I was surprised at the directness of this glance, after Carstairs's exhibition of nervousness. Apparently it was entirely intelligible to Ranney, for he set his jaw with grim determination, and proceeded to answer the coroner.

"I was wakeful off and on, all night, sir. I can't say as I was awake at twelve o'clock, and I can't say as I wasn't. I'm a light sleeper, sir."

"Then you would have heard if anything unusual was taking place?"

"Do you mean here at the house, sir? Because my cottage is too far away for me to hear burglars or anything like that."

"Did you hear or see anything unusual at any time during the night?"

Again Ranney hesitated, again he looked at CarStairs, this time including Mrs. Carstairs in his glance.

To my surprise, while the valet still had a threatening aspect, his mother smiled slightly at Ranney. It was a strange smile, a little coaxing and of a persuasive charm.

I don't know whether anyone else noticed this by-play, and the detective paid no attention to it whatever, but it interested me. And I thoroughly believed that it was in response to Mrs. Carstairs's beseeching glance, that Ranney said, firmly:

"No, sir, nothing did I hear or see all night long."

I didn't believe him. To me it was a palpable untruth, but I saw a quiet smile of satisfaction on Mrs. Carstairs's face, and a victorious gleam in the eyes of her son. What it all meant, I didn't know, and I began to think perhaps I was making too much of it, when suddenly I remembered Miss Fordyce's account of the motor car and the man she had seen from her window. Could Ranney or Carstairs know anything about this, and did it bear on the mystery? I glanced at Miss Fordyce, but she still sat with closed eyes, and looked like one in a trance. I doubted if she had even heard Ranney's evidence, or that of the valet.

But I argued to myself that it would be wiser for me to say nothing, and wait until the testimony of Miss Fordyce should be called for; when she would have to tell about the motor car, and I could then see if either of these servants showed any guilty knowledge.

Next came the evidence of the doctor. He deposed that he had been the Van Wyck family physician for a great many years. He told of being called that morning to Buttonwood Terrace, and of his seeing the body of David Van Wyck. It was his opinion after examination that Mr. Van Wyck's death occurred about midnight.

"From what cause?" asked the coroner. "I frankly admit," said Doctor Mason, "that I am puzzled as to the instrument which caused Mr. Van Wyck's death. I have made an examination of the body, and I find no bullet or shot. I conclude, therefore, that he was stabbed with some sharp, pointed instrument which has left a small circular hole in the clothing and the flesh."

"Could it have been a hat-pin?" asked the coroner.

"No, it could not," declared the doctor, a little shortly. "I don't know why people are so ready to assume a hat-pin. As a matter of fact, a hat-pin is a most impracticable weapon. It would either bend double or break off if used for such a purpose. Nor was it a dagger—of any usual description. A dagger or a knife would leave a slit-like incision, and the mark in question is absolutely circular. I can only say that the weapon must have been sharppointed and round. Further than that, I do not know."

"Could the wound have been self-inflicted?" asked the coroner.

"So far as its position is concerned, yes; but it is improbable that a man could have sufficient force of nerve to stab himself in that manner, for it meant a sure, strong drive of the weapon. Also, it is improbable that after that thrust the victim could live long enough to draw out the weapon and hide or dispose of it. And I understand it has not been found."

"No," returned Mr. Mellen; "it has not yet been found, but it may be eventually discovered. It is your opinion, then, Doctor Mason, that David Van Wyck was not a suicide?"

"That is my opinion," returned Doctor Mason positively.

Chapter 10: Further Evidence

NEXT came Barclay Lasseter, the secretary.

"Your name and position?" asked the coroner, curtly.

For some reason the young man showed rather a defiant attitude.

"I am Barclay Lasseter, and my position was that of secretary to David Van Wyck."

"Confidential secretary?"

"Yes, private and confidential secretary."

"For how long have you held that position?"

"A little over a year."

"What are your duties?"

"My duties have been, to do whatever Mr. Van Wyck required of me in the way of attention to his correspondence and business affairs."

"You live here?"

"No; I board in the village. But frequently, at Mr. Van Wyck's request, I've stayed here over night, or for a few days at a time."

"When were you last with Mr. Van Wyck?"

"Last evening, when a committee of three gentlemen visited him in his study."

"For what purpose?"

"It was Mr. Van Wyck's intention to make a gift of nearly a million dollars for a village library, and three prominent men of the village were a committee to accept this gift and superintend its disposal as directed."

This evidence caused a decided sensation in the audience. The library plan had been a secret until now, and the village people were astounded at the news. The coroner went on:

"As confidential secretary you must know all about the details of this plan for the library."

"I only know that it was Mr. Van Wyck's positive intention to make the gift. Papers were drawn up to that effect last evening, but they were not completed and not signed."

"And those papers have been stolen?"

"They have disappeared."

"Meaning that Mr. Van Wyck may have disposed of them himself, before he died?"

"Meaning nothing, but that the papers are missing, and I have no way of ascertaining whether they were stolen or not."

"And the Van Wyck pearls? They are also missing?"

"They are."

"They were always kept in the safe?"

"Not always, but usually."

"When not in the safe, where were they?"

"In the possession of Mrs. Van Wyck."

"Did she prefer to keep them in her own possession?"

This question seemed to me too personal, and I noticed both Archer and Morland showed frowning faces at the coroner's words.

But Lasseter answered decidedly: "She certainly did. The possession of the pearls was a constant source of disagreement between them."

This roused me to extreme indignation, but as I looked at Anne, and saw the calm, even supercilious expression on her face, I concluded I was too sensitive in the matter, and probably it was necessary that these things should come out in the evidence. I knew David Van Wyck's disposition, and it was not at all astonishing that he and Anne should have quarrelled about the pearls. I knew they were hers in the sense that he had given them to her. But I knew, too, that he claimed the ownership of all and any of her property. However, it was very ungracious of Lasseter to volunteer the information as to marital disagreements.

"When did you last see Mr. Van Wyck alive?" Mr. Mellen next inquired of the witness.

." I was present at his conference with the committee. Those gentlemen stayed until well after eleven. I then remained with Mr. Van Wyck until very nearly twelve, leaving for home, I should say, at about ten minutes before midnight."

"You left Mr. Van Wyck's study, and went directly to your home?"

"I did," returned Lasseter, and, though the answer was prompt, there was something about the man's voice that made me doubt his integrity. I had no reason to question the truth of his statement, but his wandering eye, a certain nervous working of his features, and his restless clasping and unclasping of his hands made me wonder whether or not he had anything to conceal. But I also realized that the curt, almost aggressive manner of Coroner Mellen was enough to disturb the poise of the most innocent witness.

"You left Mr. Van Wyck alone in his study?"

"Not so. His son, Morland, was with him."

"I was not!" declared Morland, starting up from his seat not far from me.

Lasseter paid no attention to this interruption, and the coroner said, "Why does Mr. Morland Van Wyck contradict you, Mr. Lasseter?"

"I don't know," said the secretary. "I repeat that when I left the study, I left Mr. Van Wyck and his son there, and I said good-night to both as I went out of the door."

"Did they respond to your good-night?"

"The elder Mr. Van Wyck said, 'Good-night, Lasseter,' in his offhand way, and immediately followed it with a remark to his son."

"What was the remark?"

"He said, 'You see, Morland, I have proved that I could carry out my intention, after all.' "

"And did Mr. Morland Van Wyck reply to this?"

"That I cannot say, as I was by that time outside the door and had closed it behind me."

"And you know nothing more of this matter?"

"The next time I saw Mr. Van Wyck was when I arrived here this morning and found him dead."

"You are positive that when you left last night Mr. Morland Van Wyck was in the study with his father?"

"I am positive."

There was a breathless silence. It was quite evident from the expressions on the faces of the audience that they had leaped to the conclusion that Morland Van Wyck had killed his father because of the plan for endowing a library. The villagers had become aware of the situation so suddenly, and had been so astonished at the munificence of the gift, that it seemed to them but natural that the Van Wyck family should resent this disposal of a fortune. But the thought of Morland committing a crime because of it appalled them, and looks of horror could be seen on every face. Morland Van Wyck was next called as a witness.

The sight of his livid, angry face seemed to render the coroner incapable of definite questions,

"What have you to say for yourself?" he said.

"I have this to say," thundered Morland: "Barclay Lasseter lies when he says he left me with my father! The truth is, I left the study before Lasseter did. I left him there with my father, and if he states the contrary, he has his own reason for doing so!"

"You are implying--" began the coroner.

"I'm implying nothing!" Morland stormed on.

"I am stating that I left my father and his secretary alone in the study. And I am stating nothing but that." He threw a defiant look at the secretary, who returned it in kind. Coroner Mellen was decidedly nonplussed. He seemed to fear an outbreak of personal hostilities between these two, and he said hastily, "Let us not pursue this further. One of you gentlemen must be mistaken. Mr. Van Wyck, have you any opinion or theory as to the cause of your father's death?"

I thought this rather clever of the coroner, for it would bring forth either an accusation of the secretary or a tacit implication of freedom from suspicion.

"My opinion is the only one possible to hold. My father was murdered by some evil-minded intruder. Presumably an expert burglar, because valuable jewels and valuable papers have been stolen."

"But how, in your opinion, could this intruder commit his crimes and get away, leaving the room securely locked and bolted on the inside, with no possible means of ingress or egress?"

"I'm not prepared to say how he did it; the fact remains that he did do it."

At this point a juryman made a remark. He was a shrewd-faced young fellow, and seemed imbued with a sense of his own importance.

"I wish to say," he began, "that we should like at least a suggestion as to how the murderer could have escaped from a room which we may call hermetically sealed."

Morland turned on him with an impatient gesture. "I hate that term 'hermetically sealed'! It is absurd, to begin with. That my father's murderer did get out of the room is proved by the fact that the instrument of death cannot be found. Therefore, since the murderer did get out, the room cannot be hermetically sealed, however much it may appear so."

"Can there be any secret or concealed entrance?" asked the alert juryman.

"No," replied Morland; "there is nothing of that sort in the house. And the study is really a separate building, only attached at one corner. Moreover, a burglar, however enterprising, could hardly know of a secret entrance of which we did not know ourselves! I tell you, Mr. Coroner, the murderer got away after the clever fashion of a cracksman who knows his business. How he did it, I cannot tell you; but he killed my father, stole the Van Wyck pearls, stole also the deed of gift which had been drawn up for the village library, and then escaped.

Escaped, Mr. Coroner, and is therefore still at large! But he must be found, and no effort must be spared to find him!"

I looked at Morland in astonishment. He had assumed a rather pompous attitude and seemed to be giving orders instead of giving evidence. Coroner Mellen looked greatly disturbed. I felt sure that he was beginning to realize that the case was more than he could cope with. His limited intelligence could not grapple with the mysteries and contradictions that confronted him.

Also, he began to realize that Morland had a high temper, and that if aggravated much further he might create an unpleasant scene.

"We are even now using our best efforts to discover the criminal, Mr. Van Wyck," Mr. Mellen went on. "And I count upon you for assistance in the matter."

"How can I assist you?" Morland blazed. "If I knew anything at all about the matter I should volunteer the information, without having it dragged out of me! You must hold your inquest, of course; but it will tell you nothing, for the problem is too deep and too mysterious to be solved easily. We have engaged a detective in whom I have confidence; but the truth cannot be learned by questioning witnesses. However, Mr. Coroner, proceed with your duties and get them over as soon as may be."

"That is what I am doing," said Mr. Mellen, with a sudden accession of dignity. "And in order to proceed properly, I must insist upon asking you some further questions, even at the risk of being considered personal. Were you on good terms with your father at the time of his death?"

"What!" thundered Morland. "Of course I was! I have never been on anything but good terms with my father. To be sure we've had differences of opinion, and we never hesitated to state plainly our views to each other, but I don't call that being on bad terms with him. In case of a disagreement we fought it out as man to man. Naturally, I objected to his foolish plan of founding a library of proportions and values altogether too great for a tiny village like Crescent Falls. Naturally I told him so. As he was very determined in the matter, we had high words on various occasions; and last night matters came to a climax."

"What do you mean by came to a climax?"

The coroner fairly pounced on this phrase.

"I mean what I say! The climax of my father's plan was reached, when he called the committeemen to meet him and accept his absurd gift! I do not blame these gentlemen. They would have been foolish, indeed, to refuse a gift so freely offered to them. I was present myself at the interview, and I used every argument I could think of, to dissuade my father from his project. But I think I may say, and I think the gentlemen of the committee will bear me out in this, that every objection I raised, only made my father more determined to have his own way."

The three men who had represented the committee were all present, and they nodded their heads in confirmation of Morland's statement.

I looked at Morland thoughtfully. At one moment I would feel convinced that he was really a good son, and that it was beyond belief that he should have raised his hand against his own father. And then I realized his ungovernable temper, and his uncontrollable fits of passion, and knowing that last night had been indeed the climax of the whole subject, I wondered if a sudden spasm of passion could have made Morland so beside himself with rage, that he was almost irresponsible, and had in a frenzy committed the awful deed. And then rose in my mind the old question; even supposing he had, how did he get out of the locked room? It seemed to me that the theory of murder was impossible, unless we could discover some means of exit from that sealed study.

Mr. Mellen looked very much perturbed. He seemed unwilling to accuse Morland, and he had no evidence whatever against him. There was a breathless silence in the room, and I could not blind myself to the fact that there was a hostile atmosphere toward young Van Wyck. It was quite evident, too, that he noticed this himself, and assumed a defiant air in consequence. His whole nature was touchy, and it was characteristic of him to show bravado when an accusation was even implied.

Coroner Mellen looked at him intently and seemed uncertain what to do next.

But he must proceed, and so, with a baffled air, he dismissed Morland and called Barbara Van Wyck. The girl took the stand with no apparent trepidation, and calmly awaited questioning.

"What can you tell us of this affair?" asked the coroner briefly.

"I can tell you no facts that you do not already know," returned Barbara, in even tones and with perfect poise of manner. "But I wish to advance a theory totally different from my brother's. To repeat the phrase already used, my father's study was 'hermetically sealed.' It was impossible for an intruder to«get in and out again, leaving the room as we found it this morning. I myself examined the windows and doors, and I assure you that not only are the locks and bolts especially strong, but they are so complicated as to make it impossible to manipulate them from the outside. I hold, therefore, that my father was not murdered, but that he took his own life."

"And the robberies?" suggested the coroner. "There were no robberies. The pearls have disappeared, but I am positive that my father hid them, and that they will yet be discovered. The deed of gift he doubtless destroyed himself, and then took his own life. My father was a very eccentric man, and it is my opinion that at the last his brain gave way, and for what he did he was not mentally or morally responsible."

There was something in the girl's words and manner that carried conviction. Her quiet, dignified composure was so different from Morland's belligerent insistence that the sympathy of all present seemed to go out to her.

All over the room heads were nodding approval of her theory, and it seemed quite in keeping with the erratic career of David Van Wyck.

"But, Miss Van Wyck," said the coroner, and he seemed to speak with a certain diffidence, "if your theory is right, what became of the weapon used by your father?"

"I do not know, nor do I know what that weapon could have been. But I hold that that may yet be discovered, and I hold too that the absence of that weapon is not so inexplicable a mystery as is the question of how a burglar could escape from that room."

This was true so far as it went. We were confronted by two seeming impossibilities: if a suicide, the weapon could not have disappeared; if a murder, the murderer could not have made his exit from that sealed room. As theories, one might take one's choice!

"You think, then," Mr. Mellen was saying, "the missing pearls will yet be found?"

"I do not know," replied Barbara. "I think that my father hid them with the unnatural cunning of a diseased mind. For I am perfectly certain that my father was not sane when he took his own life. And if the same ingenuity which marked the manner of his death prompted his hiding of the pearls, it may well be possible that we shall never find them." I looked at Miss Van Wyck in amazement. The girl I had thought so colorless and inane was proving possessed of an unsuspected strength of character. Her simple, logical statements carried great weight, and, though she left unsolved a principal point, many of her listeners showed a decided willingness to subscribe to her theories.

CHAPTER 11: ARCHER'S THEORY

FOR some reason best known to himself, the coroner next called upon the three men who formed the village committee. These were Mr. Millar, Mr. Brandt and Mr. Garson. As he had been chairman of the committee, Mr. Brandt was chosen to speak for the three.

The witness was a middle-aged and dignified-looking man of a fine presence. He told in a straightforward manner of the proposed gift from Mr. Van Wyck to the village. He said further that the committee thought the project was extravagant, and they felt much hesitation on accepting the library. But, he said, the more they demurred, the more insistent Mr. Van Wyck became. And he finally persuaded them that they had no right to refuse so valuable an institution for their village, and so, he concluded, they had decided to accept it and had come the night before to attend to the formalities.

It was clearly impossible to connect these gentlemen in any way with the crime, but I surmised that Mr. Mellen hoped to get some important evidence from them. He questioned Mr. Brandt closely as to the attitude and behavior of Morland Van Wyck during the evening, and also inquired concerning the secretary.

But Mr. Brandt said nothing enlightening. He admitted that the Van Wycks, father and son, had discussed the project hotly, he even admitted that the discussion could properly be called a quarrel. Of the secretary he had nothing to say, as he had merely performed clerical duties and took no part in the actual business of the meeting.

The necessary papers, constituting the Deed of Gift had been drawn but not signed. For technical reasons they had been left over night in the possession of Mr. Van Wyck, who had said he would put them in his safe.

Mr. Brandt further testified that the three committeemen had left at about quarter after eleven, and that Mr. Van Wyck had bidden them a hearty and pleasant good-night. Mr. Brandt spoke for his committee in expressing regret that the Deed of Gift was missing. And indeed it was quite evident that that regret occupied the minds of the three men almost to the entire exclusion of the more tragic happening.

This shocked me, until I remembered that they were only slightly acquainted with David Van Wyck, and even that acquaintance was not of a friendly character. Perhaps, then, it was not to be wondered at that they felt more keenly the loss of the projected gift than the loss of its giver. I was secretly glad that the Deed of Gift was lost, although being unsigned it was probably valueless. But since David Van Wyck was dead, I felt a decided satisfaction that his fortune must necessarily remain in his own family instead of being given away.

Next to give evidence were the guests of the house. Mrs. Stelton seemed almost to enjoy the importance of being questioned as a witness, and answered volubly and with an evident intention of making a good impression on the audience. She spoke to them rather than to the coroner, and showed a certain personal interest that was clearly meant to imply that she was or would some time be a permanent member of the Van Wyck household. And yet, though she cast frequent glances at Morland, they were not always responded to, nor did he seem absorbedly interested in what she was saying. Then, too, her testimony was of no importance whatever. She could tell nothing that was not already known, and her opinions were absolutely valueless. She was soon dismissed, and Beth Fordyce took her place.

As she rose from her seat and went slowly forward to the chair indicated for her, she looked so listless and distracted that I wondered if she would be able to repeat the story she had told me. I think Mr. Mellen gathered from her appearance that her evidence would not be of much importance, for after a few preliminary details, he said in a most uninterested way, "Can you tell us, Miss Fordyce, of any circumstance or evidence bearing on the case that we have not already heard?"

"I certainly can," and Beth Fordyce's blue eyes lighted up as if with a realization of her own selfimportance.

And then in a manner which amazed me, she gave a clear and definite account of the motor car, and the strange man she had seen the night before.

"And I am not sure it was a man," she said, as she came to that part of her story. "I saw only a medium-sized person with a long coat on, and as the figure crawled stealthily along in the shadow of the house, I could not discern if it might be a man or a woman."

"This is indeed most important, Miss Fordyce," said the coroner, evidently pleased to find something to work on. "It is extremely probable that the figure you saw, was that of the criminal we are seeking."

"But what good does that do," inquired Miss Fordyce, earnestly, "since you have no idea who the person could have been?"

"But we may be able to find out. At least we have a tangible clue to work upon."

The clue seemed to me a most intangible one, and I couldn't help thinking that any story of Beth Fordyce's would have to be corroborated by some one else, before it could have much weight with me. I glanced at Markham and saw that he was intently studying the face of the witness as he made a few notes on a bit of paper. Without a doubt he meant to interview her alone later. Of course the appearance of a strange motor at midnight was exceedingly important, if true. But who could say it was not one of the hallucinations or visions to which Miss Fordyce was unfortunately subject?

I looked at the others. Barbara and Morland looked frankly incredulous. They knew the girl, and I know they

thought her story might be true and might not. Anne
looked eager, as if hoping that here was at least a
beginning of the solution of the mystery. Archer looked
uninterested, and kept his eyes on Anne, as if trying to
read her thoughts. Mrs. Carstairs and her son were
greatly agitated. Mrs. Carstairs controlled it and the
valet did not. But as they had been agitated during most
of the inquest, I could not tell whether Miss Fordyce's
story had made any special impression on them or not.
And then, again, I remembered their search in the road.
Could there be any connection between their mysterious
searching and the mysterious motor car?

But Miss Fordyce was still on the witness stand. The
coroner evidently thought that she was an important
witness after all and questioned her on many subjects. In
response to one of his inquiries, she repeated a remark
which Morland had made to his father at dinner the night
before. This speech was to the effect that Mr. Van Wyck
would be sorry if he carried out his plan. I couldn't believe
that Beth intended even to cast a shadow of suspicion in
Morland's direction, but, to the eager crowd waiting for a
straw to show which way the wind blew, this speech was
indicative. And yet, quite unconscious, apparently, of
having said anything by way of suggestion, Beth took her
seat, placid and unruffled.

But to Morland, evidently the shaft had struck home.
He remembered he had said that to his father, he realized
that it might react against him. I thought of this, too, and
then I remembered that Lasseter had sworn that he had
left Morland alone with his father, and Morland had
given him the lie!

But already Archer was testifying. The gist of his
evidence was practically the same as the others, but he
related it in a concise, straightforward way that held the
attention of his hearers. He said that he had said good-
night to the ladies at about halfpast ten the night before,
and that then, in company with me, he had gone to the
smoking-room, where we stayed for perhaps half an hour,

both going to our rooms at about eleven o'clock. He then told of our meeting again at the break fast-table, and of Anne's coming to the dining-room to tell us of Mr. Van Wyck's non-appearance. Of course the rest of his story was practically a repetition of the others. "Have you any theory regarding the crime?" asked Mr. Mellen, and the oft-repeated question took on a new interest as Archer said thoughtfully:

"It's hardly a theory, but I should like to suggest an idea that may or may not be plausible."

"What is it?" asked the coroner, with interest.

"I'm afraid it will sound absurd," said Archer slowly and seriously; "but it is the only explanation I can think of, which would be even a possible solution of the mystery. Though I'm not a detective, nor can I deduce facts from circumstantial evidence or clues, yet this possibility I speak of is merely an adaptation of a story I once read. In this story, a well-known work of fiction, a young woman was found murdered; and the weapon could not be discovered, although it had left a small, round hole."Intense interest was manifest all over the room. Necks were craned to get a better view of the speaker.

The listeners fairly hung on his words, and many felt that the mystery was about to be solved. "In a word," went on Archer, "the weapon used was a sharp, slender icicle. As you may readily understand, it performed its fatal deed and then, melted, leaving no trace. As you can see, this is not only possible, but both credible and plausible. At this season there are no icicles, but I offer, merely as a suggestion, that if Mr. Van Wyck's death is a suicide, may it not be that the weapon was an icicle, shaped, let us say, by his own hand, from a piece of ice taken from the water pitcher."

"By Jove!" The whispered exclamation came from Lasseter, the secretary. He was staring at Archer, and muttering beneath his breath. "He's struck it!" he declared. "That's the only solution, and it must be the right one! Clever fellow!"

"He didn't deduce it," I whispered back to the secretary, for, to tell the truth, I was a little jealous that I hadn't thought of it myself; for I, too, had read the book in question. "He merely remembered having read of such a thing."

"All the same, he's right," returned Lasseter; "and I wish I'd thought of it!"

The coroner was greatly impressed with this new idea. He turned to Doctor Mason and asked his opinion.

The old doctor looked thoughtful. "I wouldn't say it was impossible; but you must remember, gentlemen, the hole left by the weapon in this case is small and perfectly round. Would it not be difficult to make, artificially, a smooth, round icicle, strong enough to pierce clothing and flesh, and strike the heart with a fatal blow?"

"It would be difficult," said the coroner, "but I must admit it seems to me the only solution. By the process of elimination, we must conclude that this is the truth."

"Rubbish!" exclaimed the detective, Markham, who had scant patience with the coroner's pompous manner. "Consider the facts. Let us suppose a pitcher of ice water had been brought into the room. Was it?" he looked round inquiringly.

"Yes," said Morland; "Father rang for it, and the butler brought it in."

"At what time?"

"About ten o'clock, I should say."

"Well," triumphantly went on the detective, "then I hold that after twelve o'clock there would not be sufficient ice left in the pitcher from which to make this deadly icicle!"

Doctor Mason nodded his head, and, indeed, we all felt that the icicle theory was rather untenable. "Well," said Archer, "it is merely a suggestion toward the explanation of the mystery. It may or may not be the correct solution. But what seems to me more important is to learn who was the last person to see Mr. Van Wyck alive. The absence of that deed of gift seems to me a very peculiar feature. A burglar would take pearls or money, but he would have no reason for taking that deed."

The coroner looked thoughtful. "If Mr. Van Wyck was murdered," he said, "there must have been a motive for the deed. It is true that a burglar would desire only money or valuables. We must conceive, then, the deed being done, that the murderer—if it is a murder—must have been some one interested in keeping Mr. Van Wyck's fortune away from the library."

The coroner had only put into words what everybody present had been uneasily thinking. The missing deed seemed to prove that the murderer was one of the household. For who, except the members of the family, would care whether Mr. Van Wyck gave away his money or not.

Of course my glance flew straight to Anne, to see how she took this blow. She sat very still, and her face was white even to the lips. I could see it was only by a brave exercise of will-power that she kept herself from collapse. Morland looked angry and belligerent. He glared at Lasseter, and the secretary responded with a stare equally unfriendly. Barbara looked horror-stricken. She seemed about to speak, and then shut her lips tightly, as if determined to say nothing at this crisis. In agony, my heart cried, "Anybody but Anne!"

I was unable to keep still. "Nonsense!" I exclaimed. "You are theorizing without data. Your implication is unwarranted and false."

The coroner looked at me, not reprovingly, but as if deeply interested. Then he dismissed Archer from the stand.

Chapter 12: Anne's Testimony

MRS. VAN WYCK was next called to testify. If Barbara had appeared calm and composed, the same could not be said of Anne. She was white and trembling to the very lips; she tottered as she walked, and with an audible sigh she sank into the chair placed for her. But all this, at least to my mind, in no way impaired her strange, eerie beauty. Her large gray eyes looked almost black against the whiteness of her pallor, and as she swept a mournful, unseeing glance round the room, I endeavored to intercept her gaze and give her a nod of sympathy and help. But she did not look at me, and, clasping her hands in her lap, prepared to meet the ordeal of the coroner's questions.

Mr. Mellen looked at her for a moment before he spoke, and his hard face took on a slightly softer expression at the sight of her evident distress. In what he doubtless meant to be a gentle voice, he said, "When did you last see your husband alive, Mrs. VanWyck?"

To my surprise, Anne showed a decided agitation. She clasped her hands tightly to her breast, and in a choked, almost inaudible voice she replied, "When he left me after dinner, to go to his study."

"He was then in good health and spirits?" asked Mr. Mellen, and a more inane question I never heard. It seemed perfunctory, as if the man scarcely knew how to broach the subject.

For a moment Anne simply stared at her questioner, as if trying to control her voice. Then she said, "My husband was in perfect health, and—yes, I think I may say he was in good spirits."

"What were his last words to you as he left you?"

If this were a random shot, it was certainly a peculiar coincidence. For we all remembered how, as he left the room, David Van Wyck had whispered to his wife something that had caused her the deepest emotion.

Anne's great eyes looked at each of us in turn. After the briefest glance at the others, she gazed longer at Archer. It may have been my imagination, but I thought he gave to her an almost imperceptible negative shake of his head. She looked frightened, and then her glance met mine. I so feared that any appearance of secrecy on her part would be prejudicial to her, that I nodded my head affirmatively, meaning for her to answer the question.

"Must I tell that?" she asked in a pained voice.

"Yes," said Mr. Mellen; "especially if it has any bearing on Mr. Van Wyck's death."

But Anne did not hear the coroner's words. She was nerving herself for her reply, and she said in a low voice, but distinctly, "As he left me, my husband whispered to me that he would give the Van Wyck pearls as well as his gift of money to the library committee."

A wave of indignation swept over the audience. Anxious as the villagers were for the gift of the library, not one of them would have wished Anne Van Wyck's jewels sacrificed in its cause. Elated by the sensational answer, the coroner continued. "Did he say anything more?" he inquired.

"Must I tell that?" Anne scarcely breathed, her face as white as the handkerchief she held.

And the coroner said inexorably, "Yes."

Had Anne looked toward me then, 1 should have shaken my head, for I feared from her expression that the revelation would be a startling one. She looked dazed, she spoke almost as one in a trance, but she said clearly, "He said, ' Now don't you wish I was dead? ' "

Doubtless it was unconscious and involuntary, but Anne had reproduced almost exactly the jeering tones of David Van Wyck's sarcastic voice, and not one of us doubted that those were the very words and the very inflection that had sounded in her ear as he had whispered to her just before leaving the drawing-room. I well remembered the agonized expression on her face as he turned away from her, and I knew that at this moment she was vividly seeing a picture of the scene.

The audience fairly rustled with this new sensation. The coroner seemed spurred, and with great enthusiasm continued his catechising.

"Why did he say that?" he said bluntly. "Had you wished him dead?"

A murmur of indignation was heard from the audience, and both Archer and Morland started as if about to protest.

But Anne raised her clear eyes to the coroner's face, and said coldly, "No, I had never wished such a thing."

"Why, then, did he speak that way?"

"Mr. Van Wyck was quick-tempered and very sarcastic of speech," she replied. "I can only explain his remark by assuming that it was prompted by anger and sarcasm."

"Mr. Van Wyck was angry, then?"

"Yes, he was angry."

"At what?"

"He was angry because the members of his family were opposed to his plan of giving away practically all his fortune to a public institution."

"And then Mr. Van Wyck left you, and you never saw him again alive?"

"That—that is so."

Except for a slight hesitation, the statement was direct, but it was manifestly untrue. Anne's eyes fell, the color came and went in her cheeks, her foot tapped nervously on the floor, and she was rapidly tying her handkerchief into knots. A more agonized, indeed a more guilty, demeanor could not have been manifested.

At that moment my eyes met hers, and it flashed across me that she and I had looked in at the window of the study and had seen Mr. Van Wyck in colloquy with the committee. Perhaps it was telepathy that carried the same thought to her, for she said suddenly, and I know she spoke truly, "Oh, yes, I did see him again after that! I was walking on the terrace later, and I saw him through the study window, talking with his visitors."

"At what hour was this?" inquired the coroner, as if the exact time of the incident were the turningpoint of the whole case.

"I don't know," returned Anne carelessly. "Perhaps about half-past nine or quarter of ten, I should say."

Mr. Mellen looked a little crestfallen, as if an important bit of evidence had gone wrong. To my mind, he certainly was a block-head, but, after all, he was merely there to ask questions, and, if the jurymen desired, they could supplement his inquiries. I glanced at the detective, Markham, to see how he took it. He was exceedingly attentive to what was going on, and sat with his head slightly forward and his eyes alert, apparently gleaning more information than was offered by the mere spoken words.

"And then," pursued the coroner, "after that glimpse through the window, you never saw your husband again alive?"

Anne answered this in the negative, but so low and uncertain was her voice that she was obliged to repeat it twice before the coroner was satisfied with her reply. I felt a vague alarm. If Anne were speaking the truth, why should she act so strangely about it? And if, by any chance, she was not veracious, she must know that her manner was unconvincing. I had no interest in any one else who might be implicated in the tragedy, but my heart again cried out, "Anybody but Anne!"

"At what time did you retire, Mrs. Van Wyck?" went on the questioner.

"I went to my room about half-past ten o'clock."

"And you retired then?"

"I did not. I read for a time, and wrote some letters, and went to bed about midnight. Or perhaps it was later—I dare say it was one o'clock."

"Are you not sure?"

"No, I didn't notice the time. Perhaps my maid can tell you. She was with me."

So casual was Anne's manner now that the coroner seemed to realize his questions were not of particular importance, and he tried a new tack.

"Was your husband kind to you, Mrs. Van Wyck?"

Anne stared at him coldly for a few seconds, and then spoke with great deliberation: "I decline to answer such a question, and I'm sure you are overstepping your rights in asking it."

Her manner even more than her words abashed the coroner, but to cover his chagrin he became insistent. "It is necessary that I should know if there was harmony between you," he declared. "I regret that the circumstances make it necessary for me to press the question."

Anne's eyes flashed. Her agitation was gone now, and her poise and calmness seemed to disconcert her inquisitor even more than her embarrassment had.

"There was perfect harmony between us," she said, holding her head proudly and looking straight at the coroner, "with the exception of this matter of the library. I tried to dissuade my husband from his intent, for his own sake quite as much as for my own, for I felt sure he would regret such quixotic generosity. But he was determined to proceed in his plan, in spite of my protests."

"And at the last moment he decided to add the valuable jewels to his gift?"

"Yes; his words to me last evening were the first intimation I had had that he meant to give away the Van Wyck pearls."

"Had you any reason to doubt your husband's sanity?"

"None, except in this matter of the library gift. Nor do I call that insanity; but rather a monomania which possessed him temporarily."

"Do you think your late husband hid the pearls, or do you think they have been stolen?"

"I can form no opinion, as my husband's death is so wrapped in mystery. He may have secreted the pearls or they may have been stolen by an expert burglar. Personally, I have no theories on the subject. It is all utterly mysterious to me."

Anne passed her hand wearily across her brow with a gesture of exhaustion. I think this roused the coroner's sympathy, and he excused her from further questioning.

Mrs. Carstairs was next called as a witness. There was a stir among the audience as she rose and walked slowly to the witness chair.

It was quite evident that considerable curiosity was felt regarding this woman.

I expected she would appear perturbed, but instead, she had a calm air of superiority and held her head high as if entirely mistress of the situation. In spite of myself, I was obliged to admit that her face was fascinating in its expression, quite apart from the real beauty of her features. And then I suddenly realized that this remarkable woman was deliberately trying to charm the coroner by her demeanor!

She was beautifully gowned, as always, in black lustreless crepe de chine, which clung to her beautiful figure in long sinuous lines and which, to my imagination, gave her the effect of a beautiful serpent. Her personality affected me unpleasantly and yet absorbed my attention entirely. She was so evidently conscious of the effect she produced, that it was as interesting as a play to watch her.

The very way in which she sat in her chair was a picture of itself. But it was no strained or forced pose, merely the careless grace of a perfectly poised woman. I glanced at Anne, and was surprised to see that she, too, was looking at Mrs. Carstairs admiringly. The two women were deadly enemies at heart, and it seemed to me to indicate a fine, generous nature in Anne to forget her prejudice in an honest appreciation of the other's charm.

Mr. Mellen looked at his witness a little uncertainly. Clearly he did not understand Mrs. Carstairs, and was not sure how to address a woman of this type.

After the preliminary questions, as to her position and length of sojourn in the family, he said, almost abruptly:

"Do you think Mr. Van Wyck was a suicide?"

"It may be," replied Mrs. Carstairs, in low, musical tones. "Mr. Van Wyck had reason to wish to die. And there are those who wished him dead." As she said these words, Mrs. Carstairs dropped her eyes and sat quietly awaiting further questions. Her speech almost amounted to an accusation, and Morland looked at her with a face full of rage and with clenched hands.

"Will you explain that implication, Madam?" asked the coroner.

"It was no implication, it was merely a statement."

"Very well, then, amplify it. Who are those, who, in your opinion, wished the death of David Van Wyck?"

Mrs. Carstairs assumed an expression of gentle pathos, which, while beautiful to behold, seemed to me the quintessence of hypocrisy. In a sad, low voice, she said, slowly:

"A man's foes shall be they of his own household."

Mr. Mellen stared at her. "It is your opinion, then," he said, "that David Van Wyck's death may have been brought about by some one who lived under this roof?"

"Do you not think so?" and the question was accompanied by a grave look, of infinite pain. "You are here to answer questions, not to ask them. Nor are you invited to give unsupported opinions. If you know of anything, madam, definite and positive, that would lead

you to suspect the thing you mention, tell us of it at once.
But if not, kindly refrain from insinuation or implication."

Mrs. Carstairs looked amazed rather than reproved.
To my mind, she was suddenly confronted by a man who
could not be cajoled by her fascinations, and who was
outspoken in reply to her veiled hints.

"Assuredly I know of nothing definite, or I should
have divulged it sooner."

"To your knowledge, had Mr. Van Wyck an enemy in
his own household?"

"Enemy is a harsh word. But the man was far from
happy with one who should have been his closest friend."

"Meaning his wife?"

"Meaning his wife." Mrs. Carstairs's face was white,
now, and her eyes had a steely glitter as she said these
words, looking straight at the coroner.

"You state, then, that Mr. Van Wyck was not happy in
his marital relations?"

"I state that, emphatically." There was a murmur of
disapproval all through the room at the trend of this
conversation, and more than one was heard to whisper,
"Shame!" and, "This won't do!"

I could see that Archer, Morland and the others were
restrained from speech only by Anne herself. As I had
noticed before when these two women clashed, Anne won
by the force of her marvellous aloofness. She now sat
regarding Mrs. Carstairs with an expression of slight
scorn, which said far more strongly than words could
have expressed, that the witness was talking nonsense.
Anne Van Wyck looked like a queen listening to the
prattle of a demented subject, and her absolute
indifference to the housekeeper's remarks was the one
reason why her friends did not at once put a stop to the
testimony. I saw at once that Anne's attitude was the
best possible refutation of the housekeeper's evidence;
and I saw, too, that Mrs. Carstairs was herself quite
aware of this. I think Anne's look of supercilious scorn,
almost tinged with amusement, acted as a whip to the

housekeeper's burdened soul, and spurred her to greater effort.

"I know of what I am speaking," Mrs. Carstairs went on, "for David Van Wyck was engaged to me, when he met and wooed the lady he made his wife." She flashed a dazzling smile at the coroner, which went far to disturb that gentleman's equilibrium.

"It was then—it was then, a breach of promise?" he said, half involuntarily.

"It was,—yes. But of course I never sued him, or in any way asserted my rights. He was sufficiently punished by his unhappy marriage. His wife has always been jealous of me. She has endeavored many times to have me dismissed from my position, but with no success. However," and here Mrs. Carstairs turned her direct gaze upon Anne, "since the death of her husband, Mrs. Van Wyck has asserted her intention of getting rid of me! I accuse no one. I only state that there are several who would consider themselves benefited by the death of David Van Wyck."

The quiet intensity of the speaker's voice took away the melodramatic effect of the scene, and made her seem like an accusing angel speaking words of Fate.

There was a pause which was broken by Detective Markham, who burst out, with something the effect of a bomb-shell: "And your son is one of them!"

At last something had disturbed Mrs. Carstairs's calm. She turned white to the very lips, and she trembled as if mortally afraid. But she made a brave effort to control herself, and said, distinctly, though in tones that quivered, "My son is in no way implicated!"

"Then what were you searching in the road for, early this morning?"

"I was not searching " began Mrs. Carstairs, and then, as she saw me looking intently at her, she stopped speaking.

"You were," declared the detective; "there's no use your denying it! And later on, your son was seen

searching in the same place. What clue was he looking
for?"

Mrs. Carstairs could not speak. Her lips moved
inaudibly, but she was striving to pull herself together
and would doubtless have succeeded, when, breaking the
silence, the voice of Beth Fordyce was heard.

It sounded weird, and the audience listened
breathlessly as Beth said, in dreamy, far-away tones,
"Wheel tracks! He was looking for wheel tracks! He was
the man who came in the motor car! I recognize him
now,—it was Carstairs, Mr. Van Wyck's valet, who came
into the grounds, at midnight, in a motor car. Who
stopped—and hesitated —and proceeded at intervals—
who left the car, and walked stealthily around the house
in the shadow of the eaves—evading the moonlight—
seeking the shadow—the shadow--"

Miss Fordyce's voice trailed away in a whisper, and I
knew that she was in one of the semi-trances, or
whatever word might express the strange condition that
sometimes enveloped her. She was perfectly conscious,
but her mentality seemed dual. She envisioned other
scenes than those she might be among, and while she saw
them clearly she spoke as if through a mist.

The audience sat enthralled. Here at last was a hint
of something real and tangible! Wheel tracks were
legitimate clues! If Miss Fordyce's story were true, there
was at last a way to look for light on the mystery!

I glanced at Mrs. Carstairs, expecting to find her
almost collapsed; but instead, she had again risen to the
occasion and resumed her grasp of the situation. I saw,
too, that it was the alarm of her mother instinct, that had
nerved her to a renewed effort at composure, and she said
quietly, "There is no meaning to the babble of a mind
given to frequent hallucinations?"

But apparently the coroner thought there was, for he
abruptly dismissed Mrs. Carstairs as a witness, and
recalled her son. The valet looked wretched, but seemed
ready to answer questions.

"Did you come into this place in a motor last night at midnight?" the coroner shot at him.

"No, sir," and the answer was firm, though in a low tone.

"You have testified that you were at a ball in the village."

"Yes, sir, but I walked home. It—it isn't far, sir."

"Can you prove that you were at this village ball? Did any of the servants of this house see you there?"

"N-no, sir."

"How does that happen?" snapped the coroner; "were none of them present at the ball?"

"I don't know, sir."

"What do you mean? Look here, Carstairs, you weren't at that ball at all! Where were you? Were you out in a motor?"

"No, sir; oh, no, sir!" The man's denial was so emphatic and his manner so agitated, that it was palpably a falsehood on the face of it.

"I think you were," the coroner went on, "and as I doubt your word, I will ask some one else." Then the coroner called for Ranney, the garage mechanician.

This witness doggedly persisted that he knew nothing of Carstairs's whereabouts the night before. But persistent nagging by the coroner finally drew out the fact that the new touring car had been taken out.

"How do you know it had?" asked the coroner, and Ranney seemed suddenly to decide that he would make a clean breast of the matter.

"I seen the wheel tracks, sir," he said.

"How did you know them from any other tracks?"

"It's a new car, sir, and it has peculiar tires. You can't mistake the tracks, sir."

I saw it all in a flash. Carstairs had taken the car out for a ' joy ride,' and in order to escape discovery, he had endeavored to obliterate these peculiar tire marks from the dust of the road. And without a doubt, his mother had been engaged in the same work of precaution.

The detective also jumped to these conclusions, and after a few of his questions, in conjunction with the coroner's inquiries, they forced a confession from the valet.

Carstairs's manner became sullen as he owned up to his wrongdoing. It seemed that the use of a motor car by any of the servants was a most grave offense in the eyes of David Van Wyck. And especially, to take out the big new touring car was a daring thing to do!

Seeing that the valet was not making a good story of it, his mother cleverly managed the coroner so that she told the story instead. As Ranney had divulged the secret, she admitted that her son had taken out the car the night before. She said that it was wrong, and that she did not excuse him for it; but that since David Van Wyck was no longer here to reprove or punish him, no one else had the right to do so, and that the offense was a thing of the past, and should be forgotten. She admitted that she had heard her son return in the car, and that she was so worried about his wrong deed that she had tried to eliminate any possible proof against him in the matter of the wheel tracks. But, she concluded, this had no bearing on the crime of the night before, as her son had returned about eleven o'clock and had put the car away and had then retired. She overreached herself here, because the valet had previously testified that he came home about midnight, and both Miss Fordyce and Ranney agreed that the big car had arrived at about twelve o'clock.

But when this was put to her, Mrs. Carstairs became excited again, and insisted that the hour of her son's return was of no consequence, as he had not gone to the study at all and knew nothing of the occurrences there.

"You have no right to suspect him!" she blazed out, finally; "it is wicked for you to do so!"

"We have not said we suspected him, madam," said the coroner, gravely, "but if we do suspect him, or even feel inclined to investigate his story, it is because he has not been frank in the whole matter, and neither have you.

And now I wish to ask you further, did your son know that in the will of Mr. Van Wyck, five thousand dollars was bequeathed to him, and twenty-five thousand to yourself?"

Mrs. Carstairs hesitated.

"It would be wiser for you to tell the truth," prompted the coroner, "as you know a lack of frankness has not served you well so far. Now answer my questions truly."

"Yes, we have both known of these facts for some years."

"That is all, madam," and to my surprise, Mr. Mellen dismissed the housekeeper without a further word.

I did not quite understand his attitude in the matter, but I had no time to think about it, for I was just then called to the witness stand myself, and asked to give any information I could, that might be of any assistance in solving the mystery. I had not had time to consider this new phase of the situation that included the valet's evidence, but I had previously made up my mind what I should say when called upon.

CHAPTER 13: AN ADJOURNMENT

"I CAN tell you nothing in the way of facts that you do not already know," I said, "but I wish to say that I entirely coincide with Miss Van Wyck's opinion that her father ended his own life. It is not incredible that his very erratic mind gave way at the last. Nor is it surprising that he should destroy the deed and hide the pearls under stress of sudden insanity."

"And what is your theory regarding the manner of his death?"

"I have no definite theory; but I wish to call attention to the fact that I found several shot on the floor at Mr. Van Wyck's feet."

My statement produced quite a sensation in the audience; for the suggestion of shot seemed to imply at least a possible method of the crime.

But the detective, Mr. Markham, interrupted me and said quietly: "It is not worth while, Mr. Coroner, to waste time in consideration of the shot. There is a small receptacle on Mr. Van Wyck's desk, filled with that same shot, used as a pen-cleaner. I observed that the shot found on the floor was the same, as I have no doubt it was spilled by accident."

The Coroner turned to Doctor Mason and inquired if Mr. Van Wyck's death could have been brought about by shot.

"No," replied the doctor positively. "I probed the wound and found no bullet or shot. David Van Wyck was stabbed, and the weapon was afterward withdrawn. I cannot subscribe to the icicle theory, though I do not say it would be impossible. But the deceased was most assuredly not shot."

I felt crestfallen and a little ashamed. For, having picked up the shot, I should have noticed the same among the furnishings of the desk. The coroner asked me only a few more questions, of relative unimportance, and was about to dismiss me when he added, as an afterthought, "When did you last see Mr. Van Wyck alive?"

It was the query I had been dreading. But there was nothing for it except to tell the truth. Involuntarily, I glanced at Anne, but her eyes were cast down, and she paid no heed to me.

"Of course I was with him at dinner," I said, "and after dinner he left us to go to the study. After that I saw him a moment when from the terrace I glanced in at the study window."

"You glanced in? For what purpose?"

"No particular purpose. Mrs. Van Wyck and I were strolling by, and merely chanced to look in."

"What was Mr. Van Wyck doing?"

"Conferring with the committee from the village, I assumed. We could not hear his words, of course, nor did we try to."

"What was Mr. Van Wyck's apparent attitude?"

"He seemed to be angry," I felt myself obliged to say.

"Angry at the gentlemen of the committee?"

I was indeed sorry to give this evidence, but I was forced to do it. To decline to answer would be absurd, and, after all, everybody knew that Morland and his father were at odds in the matter. So I said, "No, he was addressing his son."

"Ah! And he seemed to be angry?"

"He did."

"Then, they were quarrelling?"

"As to that, I cannot say. I merely tell you what I saw: that Mr. Van Wyck was addressing his son, and that he had the appearance of being angry."

The coroner excused me then, and, turning to Morland, said directly, "Did you quarrel with your father last evening?"

"I told him what I thought of his procedure," replied Morland. "I make no secret of the fact that I tried my best to persuade my father not to give away his fortune."

"And do you persist in your assertion that when you left your father at midnight his secretary was still with him?"

"I do," said Morland firmly.

"And you deny this, Mr. Lasseter?"

"I do," replied the secretary, quite as positively. This deadlock was a peculiar feature of the situation. Both men could not be telling the truth, and, considering Morland's greater reason for desiring that the great gift should not be made, perhaps it was not strange that many of the audience began to turn upon him the eye of suspicion.

Everybody now had testified, and the coroner began summing up.

"I have had no direct evidence," he said, "that would tend to cast suspicion on any person. I think we must all admit that since the room was locked and barred on the inside, Mr. Van Wyck's death was not a murder. I think the erratic mind of the deceased gives us reason to assume a sudden attack of insanity. I think we must agree that if it was suicide, there was no possible means or method, unless we accept the really clever suggestion of the icicle." At this point Mr. Markham interrupted the coroner.

"I think we may discard the icicle theory," he said, "as I have found the weapon with which the crime was committed. Here it is."

Stepping forward, he laid on the table in front of the coroner a small, sharp implement partly covered with brownish stains.

The coroner looked at it as if he could scarcely believe his eyes. "What is it?" he said, picking it up gingerly.

"It is an implement used in embroidering," said Mr. Markham. "It is called a stiletto, and it forms part of every lady's sewing equipment."

The audience were fairly breathless with suspense. Swayed by the slightest hint, they were quite ready to drop suspicion of Morland and turn it toward the women of the family.

"Where did you find this?" said the coroner.

"In Mrs. Van Wyck's dressing-room," returned the detective.

"Is it your property?" asked the coroner of Anne.

"Yes," she replied, after a glance at the stiletto. "It belongs in my work-basket."

"Can you account for these stains upon it?" pursued the coroner, and he showed far more agitation than did the woman he addressed.

"I cannot," she replied coldly. "I have never used it except for embroidery purposes."

Now, of course if Anne Van Wyck had used this implement for the purpose of killing her husband, she could scarcely be expected to say so. And so her flat denial carried little weight.

"Where in the dressing-room was it found?" asked the coroner.

"Hidden beneath a pile of towels in a cupboard," replied Mr. Markham.

Whereupon the coroner inquired of Doctor Mason if the stiletto would have been a possible instrument of death.

"Mr. Van Wyck was stabbed with some weapon about that size," replied the doctor gravely. "And are these brownish stains upon it stains of blood?"

"That I cannot tell without subjecting them to analysis," returned the doctor, but his hearers were impressed with the thought that he was endeavoring by delay to give Anne the benefit of the doubt.

"I think," went on the coroner, in a hesitating manner, "that this piece of evidence must change the trend of our inquiries. Mrs. Van Wyck, did you or did you not put this stiletto in the place where it was found?"

"I did not," replied Anne quietly.

"Do you know who did place it there?"

"I do not."

"Of course," said the coroner, "the discovery of this instrument in this condition does not necessarily implicate its owner. Other hands might have used it and secreted it where it was found, perhaps with the intent of diverting suspicion. Who has the care of your dressing-room, Mrs. Van Wyck?"

"My maid, Jeannette."

"Let her be summoned," the coroner ordered.

But Jeannette was nowhere to be found. She had disappeared, no one knew when or where. To the minds of most present, this looked suspicious. It was easily to be seen that the villagers were quite ready to denounce Anne Van Wyck as the slayer of her own husband. Anne had never been popular with the village people. Clever and highly strung as she was, she had found little in common with their ordinary and, to her, stupid pursuits. And now they were quite ready to believe the worst of her.

Anne herself looked supercilious and scornful. "I have no notion where my maid has gone," she stated, "but I am positive that she is in no way implicated in this tragedy. She may have gone on some errand, and will doubtless return soon. I am entirely sure she can give you no information or enlightenment as to the crime that has been committed in this house, any more than I can."

"And you can tell us nothing, Mrs. Van Wyck, more than we know already?" the coroner said, floundering a little in the complexity of his emotions.

"No," replied Anne quietly.

The coroner fidgeted uneasily, and then said, "It is impossible to carry matters further without the testimony of the maid, Jeannette. I therefore declare this inquest adjourned for a few days, by which time I trust we may have further and more definite evidence."

The jury, to a man, looked decidedly relieved, but it was a rather disappointed audience that filed slowly out of the house. To my mind, the coroner's reason for adjourning the inquest was a pretext. I think he felt sure that if the jury had had to decide then and there, they must have accused Anne of the murder. And the evidence was certainly incriminating. While I felt, with every fibre of my being, the wish and desire to hold Anne innocent, yet there was something terribly convincing of guilt in the fact of that hidden stiletto. But again, the absurdity of it! How was it humanly possible, even granting that Anne had used the fatal instrument, for her to leave the study so securely locked and bolted on the inside?

But that was the old question, and the one to which no one had an answer. But how I hoped the answer might incriminate anybody but Anne!

That evening was a strange one. As an experience of my life, I shall never forget it. The members of the household all seemed to be at cross purposes. There were a great many people about, with the result that the Van Wycks and their house guests chose the music room for themselves and denied the others admission.

In the library were gathered the coroner and Mr. Markham in confab with Mr. Van Wyck's lawyers, and some directors of the companies with which he had been identified.

The ceremony of dinner had been a great strain on us all, but now that we were by ourselves, the tension was loosened a little.

Anne was verging on the hysterical. She had borne up so long and so bravely against the onslaughts of Mrs. Carstairs that a reaction had set in, and she seemed to lose all her defensive courage. As a result, we all tried to comfort or cheer her, and avoided referring to painful subjects. Archer was gentle and deferential, but he said little to her, and seemed to content himself with watching her closely.

Barbara and Morland were in quarrelsome mood, a condition not unusual with them. Of course it was necessary they should make certain arrangements pertaining to the funeral of their father, and naturally they deferred to Anne in many matters. But Anne listlessly declined to express any opinions, and insisted that they should use their own judgment and settle all questions between themselves.

The subject of the stiletto was not so much as mentioned, and indeed, the whole great matter of the tragedy and the inquest, was not even touched upon. Beth Fordyce was the only one who seemed inclined to open the subject, and she occasionally declared with insistence that Carstairs had killed his master.

As we were awaiting the detective's investigation of the valet's affairs, we had no wish to discuss this. Or at least, if some of us had, we did not want to do it in the presence of the Van Wyck family. I made up my mind to talk alone with Archer later, but at present, I considered it my duty to do anything I might to avoid serious or tragic considerations. It seemed to me that Anne became more and more drooping, and at last I begged of her to go for a short walk on the terrace. She agreed more readily than I had hoped, and we went out together. It was an exquisite night, the air soft and balmy, and the moon overhead.

"Just for a little while, Anne," I said gently, "forget it all, can't you? A short respite from these harrowing thoughts will clear your brain and heart, and make you stronger to bear what must come to-morrow."

She spoke suddenly, repeating my words in a frightened tone: "What must come to-morrow! What do you mean, Raymond?"

I couldn't bring myself to speak of that tell-tale stiletto, so I said, "The whole dreadful business, Anne. The conclusion of the inquest, the detective work that must follow, the funeral, and all the thousand and one accompaniments of this tragedy that has come to you. Just for an hour, put it out of your mind, and I know it will help you. Let us talk of things far off and unassociated with this place. Let us talk of when we went to school together."

We had left the terrace, and were walking down a path through one of the formal gardens. She gave me a look of trust, as she said, softly, "You are very good to me, Raymond."

"I'm your friend, Anne; it is not being good, as you phrase it, to want to help you in your sadness and trouble."

"You are my friend?" she said, slowly. "Does that mean you trust me,—you have faith in me?"

"Of course I have! I trust you infinitely. I have unbounded faith in you."

Anne's voice sank to a whisper, and she tremblingly said, "You wouldn't if you knew! Oh, Raymond, that is the pity of it—you wouldn't—if you knew "

I was appalled. Not so much by her words as by the despair in her voice. Though I wouldn't admit it to myself, it was like the wail of a guilty conscience.

Like a flash, I remembered the peculiar tone of her voice when she had said to me, "I am capable of crime."

But I wouldn't believe it. Nothing could make me believe it,—not even Anne herself. "Don't talk," I said to her; "you are overwrought, to-night. You can't see things at their proper value, and you're exaggerating something to yourself. NO.W I command you," and I endeavored to be playful, "to talk about the moon. How large do you think it is?"

Anne smiled involuntarily, for she remembered, as I did, that in our school days, it had been one of our games to discuss the apparent size of the moon. But my project was unsuccessful. After a fleeting memory, Anne forgot the moon, and burst out, passionately: "Why does that woman hate me so?" I saw that it was useless to try to divert her thoughts, so I concluded to talk with her, and it seemed to me that a direct common-sense attitude would be the best for her.

"Anne," I said, "you know very well why she hates you. .You know that, whether she told the truth or not when she said Mr. Van Wyck had promised to marry her, she certainly hoped that he would do so; and when he married you instead, it is not surprising that it should anger her against you."

"It is more than that," said Anne, musingly; "she has for me an animosity beyond that of a jealous rival. She seems uncanny, sometimes, and looks at me with what I think must be the evil eye."

"Well, granted it is so, Anne, you must rise above it. However she has troubled you in the past, she cannot trouble you any more. After a short time she will go away from here and you, Anne,—you don't expect to stay on here, do you?"

"I don't know; I haven't thought about it," and Anne gave a weary little sigh. "I wish I had some one to help me decide these things. Morland and Barbara are so fiery-tempered that I can't discuss plans coolly with them. I don't know how the will reads exactly, but I suppose it is thirds. They may have Buttonwood Terrace, if they want it, I don't care. But I don't know where to go, myself." It is a tribute to my own self-control that I didn't tell her what was in my heart concerning her future welfare, but I knew from the tone of her voice that no thought of me as a factor in her future had yet entered her mind. Whether she thought thus of Archer, or not, I did not know; but surely while David Van Wyck lay dead in the house, no one could speak of love to his widow. And yet I had a brave hope that time might bring me that for which I longed with my whole heart.

"Let the future take care of itself," I responded, gently. "What I want, Anne, just now, is for you to pluck up your courage and carry yourself through the ordeal of the next few days as bravely as may be. I have seen you rise above the annoyance of Mrs. Carstairs' presence and vanquish her with your own superiority. What you have done, you can do again."

"But that was before last night!" and Anne fairly moaned in despair. "Oh, Raymond! you don't know—you don't know!"

At that moment we heard a slight sound behind us, and a dark clad form glided by. It was Mrs. Carstairs herself, and as she passed, she murmured, "But I know, Anne Van Wyck!—I know!"

She passed away as swiftly as she had come, and as silently, and I felt Anne's form grow limp and lean against me. I could have carried her to the house, but I did not wish to subject her to a possible mortification. So, instead, I grasped her arm firmly, and whispered in her ear: "Brace up! now is the time to show what you're made of! call upon your pride, your dignity, your scorn,— whatever you will —but succeed!"

The force of my voice must have nerved her, for she straightened up and walked with a steady step toward the house. I kept my hold on her arm, till we reached the door, and then, seeing one of the maids in the hall, I bade her take Mrs. Van Wyck to her room.

Then I went to the smoking-room, and though I would not allow myself even to surmise what Anne had meant by her strange words, nor what Mrs. Carstairs had meant by her threatening whisper, I said over and over from the depths of my soul, "Anybody but Anne!"

CHAPTER 14: A MYSTERIOUS DISAPPEARANCE

I FOUND Archer in the billiard room and joined him in a chat and a smoke. Though our desultory conversation could scarcely be called a chat, so uncommunicative were we both.

But there seemed to be little to say. We agreed that the mystery was inexplicable. We agreed that the criminal, if there had been one, must be tracked down. We agreed that Markham, while a shrewd man and a reasoning one, hadn't done much as yet,— but we further agreed he should be allowed more time to show his prowess.

I certainly had no intention of telling Archer what Anne had said to me out on the terrace,—nor yet what Mrs. Carstairs had said, as she so suddenly appeared and disappeared.

And if Archer had any secret information he was equally determined not to confide in me. We told each other of our intention to remain at Buttonwood Terrace for a few days after the funeral, in the hope of being of some assistance to the family. If to both of us, "the family" was merely a euphemism for Anne Van Wyck, neither of us said so.

The talk turned again to Mr. Markham, and I compared him to Fleming Stone.

"Why," said I, "Stone would have found the criminal by this time, I'm sure."

"How?" asked Archer; "there are no clues."

"But there is mystery. I once heard Fleming Stone say that mystery in a case always spurred and enthused him. I wish the Van Wycks would engage him."

"I thought somebody said he had gone West," returned Archer, moodily, blowing smoke rings into the air.

"Yes, when he was here yesterday, he said he was to start at once. But if Markham doesn't do something soon, I shall advise employing Stone. It's all very well to say Markham must have more time, and all that, but I know what a value Stone places on looking into things before the clues have been destroyed. As you very well know, Archer, he really deduced a lot of truths from that foolish fan business, yesterday, and you must admit he's unusually clever in that way."

"I never denied it; I think he is a wonderful detective. But isn't he very expensive?"

"He is, I believe; but the Van Wycks are rich, and they ought to have the best possible expert advice in this matter."

While I was speaking, Morland came into the room. The young fellow looked worn and tired, but he had his customary belligerent air, as he flung himself astride of a chair and glared at us over its back.

"I suppose we are rich, but I don't mean to throw money away on spectacular detectives! I heard what you were saying, Sturgis, and I think it's tommyrot to get in that omniscient sleuth you're talking about. My father was killed by somebody. I'm sure I don't know who did it, but if Markham can't find out, nobody can. I don't mean by that, that I consider Markham such a great detective; but I mean, that I think the case is one that can never be solved,—and perhaps it's just as well that it shouldn't be."

Young Van Wyck sighed deeply, and then frowned, as he went on: "I suppose I'm master here now, in a way. I don't mean to question my stepmother's position or authority, but I'm the man of the house, and my wishes ought to have some weight. Especially, as Mrs. Van Wyck declines to take any part in the settlement of questions that arise."

"Don't you think," I ventured, "that the services of a good detective are really necessary?"

"No!" Morland thundered; "not since that stiletto business! Good Heavens, man! Do you want to run down that clue?"

Archer looked at the speaker as if be would jump at his throat. "You mean to say--" he blazed, and then stopped, unable to voice his own meaning. I felt equally incensed, and thought it better to speak plainly.

"Morland," I said, "I wish you'd state in plain terms what you do think."

"I don't think anything! and if I did I shouldn't say it! but you must see, both of you, what it all means. And I want to shield Anne in every way I can. Oh, let's not even speak of it,—it drives me crazy to think about it!"

The boy's face,—for Morland was really not much more than a boy,—was pathetic. He was afraid to face the conclusions which the finding of that stiletto must lead to.

Not so, Archer. The older man was quiet and composed as he said, straightforwardly: "Nothing can be gained by shirking the issue. If we refuse to consider the case, others will do so. Don't you think it's wiser to learn all we can ourselves, and be ready to meet any detective on his own ground? Now look here, Morland, if you are really anxious to shield Mrs. Van Wyck from suspicion, the best way to go about it is to face that stiletto business and run it to earth. I don't believe there's anything in it."

"I wish I could think so," and Morland's eyes showed a gleam of hope. "But you fellows don't know how Anne hated the governor."

"Hush!" said Archer, sternly; "don't say such things as that!"

"But it's true," Morland insisted, doggedly.

"You fellows don't know anything about it. At first, they got along pretty well, but lately,—well, it wasn't all Anne's fault; Dad certainly made it hard for her, with his domineering ways and unjust rules. But Anne tantalized him, too. And lately they had a lot of quarrelling over those pearls. Now I'm terribly fond of Anne,—perhaps more so than I ought to be,—but I can't help seeing things as they are. Why, it was a crisis! Last night the governor was going to give away an enormous sum of money. And, whether he intended to give the pearls too, I don't know; but he told Anne that he did." Morland ceased speaking, and indeed no more words were needed. Whatever the facts, he had set forth a theory that was at least plausible. I wouldn't believe a word of it; my heart refused to harbor the faintest suspicion of Anne,—but I knew it was only my heart that refused. My brain saw clearly the logic and truth of what Morland had said, and, too, my brain refused to forget Anne's words, "I'm capable of crime."

And so, with my heart and brain in dire conflict, I couldn't speak.

But Archer spoke. In a cold even cutting voice, he said: "You are of course entitled to jump to a conclusion if you wish. You are of course at liberty to put the worst possible construction on the evidence of the stiletto. But would you mind informing us how, in your opinion, Mrs. Van Wyck accomplished the diabolical act which you attribute to her, and left the study locked on the inside?"

Morland passed his hand wearily over his brow. "I don't know," he said; "nobody knows. But you must admit that whoever did the diabolical deed, managed in some way to leave the study door locked."

"Then until you can discover how that was done," Archer went on, "I think it will be wise for you to refrain from making accusations. I'm an older man than you are, Morland, and I think I have a right to call you down, when you pursue such a dangerous course. Even though you feel sure your suspicions are correct, I beg of you do not shout them from the housetop."

"I'm not--" began Morland, but I interrupted. "The very fact that the study was left locked, so positively points to suicide that I think it would be better to let it go at that. Why not call off the detectives and insist upon a verdict of suicide.

The fact that the weapon is missing is no more inexplicable, if as much so, as how the murderer escaped."

"I'm sure I'm willing to let it go at that," said Morland, who was now pacing up and down the room with his hands in his pockets. "I'd be glad to stop investigations at once, but I doubt if that's possible."

"And then there's Carstairs," said Archer; "that chap certainly has a guilty conscience, if anybody ever had. If investigation must be made, can't it be turned in his direction? If he's innocent, it can do no harm; and if he's implicated, we ought to know it. You see he knew both he and his mother would get big benefit from the death of his master."

"At any rate, Morland," I said, rather crossly, for my nerves were on edge, "do keep your mouth shut about your suspicions. And if you're head of the house, and if your influence counts for anything, for heaven's sake direct the trend of investigation toward suicide or Carstairs or a burglar, or anybody but Anne!"

"That's well enough to say, but I'm confronted by new suspicions all the time. I have to look over my father's papers of course, and I have already found enormous bills of Anne's,—still unpaid."

"Recent bills?" asked Archer.

"Fairly so. Within a few months. I've only looked over the papers in the safe, so far. Those on the desk I'm going to tackle to-morrow. Of course they will be the most recent bills. But I daresay there'll be plenty of them. I suppose all beautiful women are extravagant."

"At any rate, Mrs. Van Wyck has money enough now to pay her own bills," I suggested, a little shortly, for I thought Morland unduly interested in the particular matter of Anne's extravagance. "That's true," said Morland, and turning on his heel, he strode out of the room.

Archer and I were silent after young Van Wyck left us, and it was but a few moments before my companion threw his half-smoked cigar into the fireplace and announced abruptly, "I think I'll turn in."

"I'm going up, too," I said, rather relieved that no further conversation was begun.

I followed Archer up the small side staircase, which led directly to our quarters, more conveniently than the grand staircase opposite.

Archer's room chanced to be directly over David Van Wyck's bedroom, while mine was over Anne's.

There were one or two rooms between, I believe, but I don't know who occupied them.

We paused for a brief word of good-night at the head of the stairs, and then turned our opposite ways. I heard Archer's door close as I was about to open my own, when I suddenly bethought myself that I had meant to ask him what he thought about those contradictory stories of Morland and Lasseter, as to which had been left-alone with Mr. Van Wyck the night before. It seemed to me that a good deal might hinge on that question, and I wanted Archer's opinion. I didn't altogether like Archer, but I was just enough to know that it was largely due to my jealousy of his friendship for Anne, and in spite of this I had great regard for his opinions, as I had usually found them logical and right-minded. I turned back and walked along the corridor. It was but a moment since we had parted, and I assumed he could not yet be disrobing.

I tapped lightly at his bedroom door, but he didn't answer, so I tapped again.

Receiving no response, I was a little surprised, but I figured that he thought it was some one else, and not wanting any further discussion that night, he was pretending to be asleep.

So I tapped again, saying in a low tone, "It's Sturgis; let me in a minute, will you?" Still, he didn't answer, and in a moment of irritation at his silence, I turned the doorknob.

The door opened, and as the room was brilliantly lighted, I stepped inside. I didn't see Archer, but across the room a door was opened into a bathroom, and I assumed he was in there.

"Beg pardon, Archer," I called out, "but I do want to see you a minute, if I may."

Still there was no reply, and feeling that the strangeness of the situation justified it, I went to the bathroom door and looked in. The light was turned on, but there was no one in the bathroom. I was bewildered, for I knew that Archer had come in, and I could not imagine what had become of him. There was a door at the farther end of the bathroom and involuntarily I opened it. However, it was only a clothes-closet, of good size, but as it contained only a few garments, I closed the door again and returned to Archer's bedroom. As he couldn't have jumped out of the window, it naturally followed that he had left his room and gone downstairs again, while I had stood for a moment in front of my own bedroom door. It didn't seem possible, for the hall was brightly lighted, and I was sure I should have seen or heard him had he passed so near me. I spoke aloud, "Archer," I said, "are you under the bed? or where? If you are, come out!"

Again I called his name a trifle louder, and then went out of his room into the hall, closing the door behind me. I walked slowly along toward my own room, pausing at the staircase to look down. At that very moment I heard the click of Archer's door, and turning, I saw him.

"Did you want me, Sturgis?" he inquired. "Was that you calling?"

I went slowly back and entered his room, and he closed the door behind us.

"Where were you?" I said, staring around curiously.

"Where was I, when?" he returned, with a slight smile.

"When I was in here a moment ago? I tapped three times and you didn't answer, so I took the liberty of entering, and you weren't here."

"Oh, I was in the bathroom," he said lightly; "what is it you want? Cigarettes?"

"But you weren't in the bathroom, for I looked in there," I persisted, ignoring his question.

He looked at me curiously. "You did!" he exclaimed. "Well I chanced to be in the clothes-closet of the bathroom. It's rather large for the limited wardrobe I brought with me, and I expect I got lost in its depths."

"But you weren't there," I said, looking straight at him, "for I looked in there."

"Then I can only say your behavior is most ill-bred, I consider you unwarrantably intrusive."

Archer's manner was distinctly haughty and his tone even offensive, but the rebuke was deserved, and I responded, "You are quite right; I beg your pardon. And now I will tell you why I came. If you don't mind discussing it, I'd like to know what you make of those conflicting statements of Morland and his father's secretary, as to which remained in the study last night after the other left."

Archer considered seriously. "I've thought over that, myself," he said; "and do you know, the thing that most impresses me in connection with that, is that it seems to prove them both innocent of any guilty knowledge of this matter."

"How so?" I said wonderingly.

"Why because if either of them were guilty,— not that I suspect for a moment that either of them is,—but for the sake of argument, let us suppose it, —or if either of them should be concealing any bit of guilty knowledge, surely he would not so flatly give the other the lie, because he would know that such a course would invite investigation. A man with a guilty conscience is plausible and endeavors to be casual. He never makes such a sensational statement and sticks to it so blatantly."

"You ought to be a detective yourself, Archer," I said, looking at him admiringly; "I think you've made a very subtle point."

"I haven't what are called detective methods," he returned, "but I do hold that reason and logic are the mainstays of the profession. However, something more is needed. For Markham has reason and logic, and yet I doubt if he will get anywhere. I suppose ingenuity and originality are needed. Of course your Fleming Stone has those. But, Sturgis," and Archer's face grew very grave, "do we want to push this matter? Neither of us is willing to voice suspicions as Morland did, but shall we not admit to each other that a cessation of all movement in the matter, might be a good thing?"

"I don't know, Archer;" and I looked at him thoughtfully; "I see the force of your suggestion, and yet— well, I want to think it over. I'll ponder on it to-night, and I know you'll do so. To-morrow let us again exchange ideas."

Archer agreed to this, though I must confess he didn't seem greatly impressed with the brilliancy of my plan, and I went off to my own room. This time I really entered it, and locked the door after me. I threw myself into an arm-chair, and proceeded to my pondering at once. But I may as well admit that my pondering began, not with the mystery of the tragedy, but with the mystery of Archer's absence from his own room that night. It was all very well for him to say that he was in the bathroom cupboard,—but I couldn't believe it, for I had looked in there and saw no one. To be sure I didn't go inside, but Archer could scarcely have been concealed behind the few coats or trousers that were suspended from rods.

Unless he had been in one of his own suit-cases or hat-boxes he couldn't have been in that closet, and the more I thought about it, the stranger it seemed. And then the jealousy lurking in my heart gave me a sudden suggestion. Archer's room was directly over David Van Wyck's bedroom. Before his marriage, David Van Wyck had used for his own bedroom the very one Archer now occupied. Could there be,—hinted my jealous heart,—a secret staircase connecting the two? Could Archer descend secretly to David Van Wyck's room, and so gain access to Anne's apartments?

It was a tawdry thought,—it was melodramatic, — but my heart was like a tinder-box, and the thought had struck a fiendish flame. I didn't believe it with my brain, but my foolish heart declared it to be the only possible explanation of Archer's mysterious disappearance.

And then another thought followed it, which made me ashamed of my evil imagination. The dead body of David Van Wyck lay in his own bedroom. Surely no man would descend to that room on a clandestine errand.

So I forced myself to believe Archer had told me the truth, and that he had been in the cupboard, and as soon as he emerged had answered my call. It was a strange circumstance, but not so strange as the bizarre explanation I had conjured up. Besides, Morland had distinctly stated there was no secret staircase or anything of the sort in the house.

But, urged my unquiet soul, did Morland know? David Van Wyck was quite capable of keeping such a secret to himself.

And then in a sudden practical mood, I seized a pencil and drew a plan of the room as it must be. On the ground floor a corridor ran between David Van Wyck's room and the south wall of the house, to give access to the study. But as the study was two stories high, having no second floor, there was no occasion for this corridor on the second floor of the house; and in Archer's room the corresponding space above the corridor, was completely filled by the bathroom and the large clothes cupboard. I knew a little of practical architecture and I proved to myself beyond doubt that there was no space for the concealed staircase I had imagined. The walls of the old house were substantial enough, but they were by no means the thickness of walls necessary to contain secret staircases or dungeons, such as those I loved to read of in Mediaeval history. I could reckon plainly from what I knew of the rooms, just how they connected with each other; and I could account for every inch of space. Moreover, if a secret staircase had led down from the bathroom or the cupboard of Archer's room, it would have dropped plumb into the corridor below, as there was simply no other place for its outlet. I thought even of a spiral staircase, such as that in the study, at the end of the musician's gallery. But, I reasoned, that was fully four feet across; and the walls, as I computed them, were in no case more than ten inches thick.

So with a certain feeling of reluctance, and yet with a sense of relief, I gave up the idea of a concealed connection between Archer's room and the room below, and turned the trend of my ponderings toward the many and complex phases of the greater mystery.

But when I finally fell asleep that night, my dreams were all of rope ladders and secret stairways, and even vague visions of an elopement on a pillioned white palfrey, with a beautiful lady, who strongly resembled Anne Van Wyck.

CHAPTER 15: WHO WROTE THE LETTER?

THE next day was Sunday. As the inquest was not to be continued, I hoped for a quiet day; but aside from the necessary arrangements for funeral appointments, there seemed to be much going on in the way of investigations. Mr. Markham had developed a tendency to question everybody, right and left, and I continually ran against him interviewing a servant, a guest or a caller.

I hung around somewhat listlessly, hoping to be permitted to see Anne; but Miss Fordyce informed me that Anne refused to see anyone except her two step-children.

I strolled out on the terrace, hoping to have a talk with Archer, but instead, I met Mr. Markham and he proceeded briskly to interview me.

I had no objection to this, as although there were a few things I knew that I intended to keep from him, I was quite willing to give him freely any other information I possessed.

But his talk after all, was a repetition of what I already knew, or a verbose disquisition on his own theories and plans.

As we talked, Mrs. Carstairs came out on the terrace, and after a cautious glance about, she glided up to us, with a mysterious air.

"May I speak to you a minute, Mr. Markham?" she said, and though I disliked and distrusted the woman, I could not help admiring her beauty and grace. She was truly unusual in her charm, and Markham beamed on her with a smile at once admiring and deferential.

"Shall I remain?" I asked,—and for the life of me I couldn't help speaking kindly to her,—" or do I intrude?"

"Not at all," she replied; "I should be glad, Mr. Sturgis, for you to hear what I have to say. I am in a dilemma, and I don't know exactly what I ought to do. I found this," and she produced a letter, which, with a hesitating air, she offered to Mr. Markham. "I hate to bring it to you," she went on, half withdrawing it as he was about to take it, "and yet, I feel it my duty to do so."

"I'm sure it is your duty, madam," said the detective as he somewhat eagerly took the letter from her hand.

I caught sight of the inscription and a fierce anger kindled within me.

"That is a letter to Mrs. Van Wyck!" I exclaimed. "You have no right to read it, Mr. Markham! Mrs. Carstairs, where did you get it?"

My vehemence seemed to frighten her, and she clasped her hands to her breast with a little fluttering motion. "Oh, have I done wrong? Shall I put it back? I thought—I thought that in a case like this, you know, it was one's duty to tell, if one found important evidence."

Of course this was enough for Markham, and he held the letter firmly, with no intention of giving it up. But I made another desperate attempt. "Mr. Markham, you shall not read that letter, without Mrs. Van Wyck's permission! Have you read it?" and I turned and glared at the housekeeper.

"I have," she said, softly, with a look of pain in her deep eyes. "Oh, believe me, I did not know it was wrong! I thought I ought to."

"And you are right, madam," said the detective,

"Mr. Sturgis knows you are right. It is only his personal feeling that makes him want to withhold the information this letter may give."

"Oh, is that it?" And Mrs. Carstairs did not glance at me, but confined her attention to Markham.

"Then you will read it, won't you, and tell me I was right in bringing it to you. I was so uncertain what to do. If Mr. Sturgis does not want to hear it, perhaps he had better go away."

In my indignation, I was quite ready to walk away rather than be a party to this disgraceful act but as she spoke, Mrs. Carstairs swept me a glance, in which, beneath its apparent frankness, I thought I caught a malevolent gleam, and I promptly decided that I preferred to know all that anyone else knew, either for or against Anne.

The letter had been opened, and without further hesitation, Mr. Markham drew the paper from its envelope.

It was a half sheet and its message was typewritten. The detective did not read it aloud, but as I looked over his shoulder, we two scanned its contents at the same time.

There was no address, no preliminary greeting of any sort, but it was dated " Friday." Then the message ran:

"To-night is the time. After the committee meeting. Don't be afraid. You can never be found out. I will protect you and look out for you." There was no signature. I read the lines twice, but even then was unable to sense their purport. I took the sheet from Markham and scrutinized it closely. Meanwhile, he examined the envelope. There could be no doubt of its genuineness. It was addressed, in typewriting, to Mrs. David Van Wyck, Buttonwood Terrace, Town, and it bore the postmark of two days before, and of the Crescent Falls Village Post-office. A postmark on the back showed that it had been mailed Friday morning and received the same afternoon. It had been opened neatly, and gave every evidence of being a letter received and read by Anne Van Wyck on Friday. And it was on Friday night that David Van Wyck had died.

The half sheet of paper was undoubtedly from the same box of stationery as the envelope, both were of good style, rather large-sized and of good quality. Mr. Markham read it over several times, and at last he said, "This is of very grave import. You did quite right, Mrs. Carstairs, to bring it to me. Where did you find it?"

"It was in a book, which lay on a table in Mrs. Van Wyck's dressing-room. I chanced to pick up the book to put it away in its place, and this letter fell out."

"And you deliberately read it!" I exclaimed, and I daresay I glared at her.

"Perhaps I ought not to have done so, Mr. Sturgis; but I can't help thinking that in such a mysterious case as we have before us now, certain conventional rules may be laid aside."

"I quite agree with you, madam," said the detective, "and I can't help thinking that this is a most important piece of evidence. Is it your habit to look after Mrs. Van Wyck's belongings?"

"It is my duty to see that her rooms are kept in immaculate order. And unless I show a certain amount of oversight, sometimes the maids become a little careless in their care of the appointments of her dressing-table and such matters. And so, as I was in there this morning on a tour of inspection, I found this letter, as I have told you."

I was absolutely crushed. I felt as if a black mantle had fallen over me like an enveloping pall. Not for a moment did I believe Anne guilty, even of complicity in her husband's death; but I realized that my refusal to believe it was based solely on my unwillingness to do so. However, the thought flashed through my mind that this letter was dangerous and it must be destroyed or suppressed. I knew, too, that Mr. Markham was ready and eager to make use of it and I concluded that the only thing I could do was to beg for time.

So I said: "I quite agree with you, Mr. Markham, that this is a serious matter. So much so, that I think you will both be willing to agree to my proposition, which is to say nothing about it for a day or two. Let us, at least, wait until after Mr. Van Wyck's funeral, which takes place to-morrow afternoon. I think it only decent courtesy that all investigation should be postponed until after that."

Mr. Markham considered this matter. "It might be well to adopt that course," he said, slowly, "though of course I shall conduct personally and privately any investigation I choose. But I'm quite willing to agree that the whole matter shall not be mentioned to any member of the family until after the funeral."

"Perhaps it need never be mentioned," said Mrs. Carstairs, and her face was drawn with sorrow.

"I'm just beginning to realize what it would mean if this discovery of mine were made public. Why, it is practically a condemnation of Anne Van Wyck!"

"It is.nothing of the sort!" I cried out, angrily. "It is doubtless a harmless communication on a totally different subject. There is really nothing to connect it with the crime in the study."

"Don't talk rubbish," said Mr. Markham, testily. "If ever a bit of evidence pointed straight to a criminal, this certainly does. There can be no doubt of its genuineness. The date and postmarks prove that Mrs. Van Wyck received this letter on Friday afternoon. The fact that it was found in a book which she had been reading, proves that she received and opened it herself. If all this is not so, what is your explanation of the incident, Mr. Sturgis?"

"Yes, do tell us," said Mrs. Carstairs, wringing her beautiful hands. "I should be so glad to put any construction on it favorable to Mrs. Van Wyck. .Would it be better to go to her and ask her frankly what it means?"

"No!" I thundered; "that poor woman is not to be harassed any more than is necessary during these awful days. You have both promised to keep this matter a secret until after the funeral and I hold you to your word."

To my relief, they both agreed to this, and promised not to mention that awful letter to any one at present.

I looked curiously at Mrs. Carstairs. As always, she mystified me, and yet I couldn't say how or why. Surely she had been guilty of a breach of good manners in reading a letter addressed to another. But in her opinion the occasion had justified it; and doubtless many people would agree with her. Really, I could not help distrusting her, in spite of the fact that she now expressed so much sympathy for Anne and seemed so truly grieved at the thought of her trouble that she seemed to be sincere. And again, what could she have done with the letter better than to bring it straight to the detective. It was the most logical proceeding and the most just.

If she had taken the letter to Morland or Barbara it might have made infinitely more trouble. I walked away, leaving the two on the terrace still conferring on the matter. As I turned aside I heard Mr. Markham say, "What was the book in which you found the letter?" And Mrs. Carstairs replied, "A Volume on Rose Culture."

The question struck me as absurd, for what difference could it possibly make what the subject of the book might be. I walked along the terrace and down into the gardens. Finding a pleasant seat on one of the by-paths I sat down there to think it over. I didn't need the letter to look at, its words were branded into my brain.

Alone by myself, I was forced to admit that the letter, if genuine, was definitely condemning. And it was genuine, beyond a doubt. Anne had certainly received that letter on Friday. The letter stated that after the committee meeting that same night was the time for some preconcerted plan to be carried out. That the plan was a dangerous one was proved by the wording of the letter. And it was shortly after that committee meeting that David Van Wyck had died a violent death.

I forced myself to face the matter squarely.

Not because I believed it, but merely as a necessary argument, I accepted the implication that the letter conveyed. Then it would mean that Anne had an accomplice, or at least an advisor in the matter.

Who could the accomplice be? But my mind refused to work in that direction, and I resolutely pushed the matter out of my mind and began to think what I could do to help and protect Anne if she should be accused. I almost thought of urging her to run away with me while she yet had opportunity to escape.

And as my thoughts were in this turmoil, Anne herself came walking along the path near me. Her soft, trailing black garments made her beautiful face seem whiter than ever.

"Sit down, Raymond," she said, as I rose; "talk to me a little, can't you? I feel dazed and weak."

Surely this was no time to ask questions, so I talked to her gently, on casual subjects, and after a time the conversation veered around to the tragedy.

"I felt a premonition something would happen that night," said Anne, her large, dark eyes growing misty with the memory. "I was so restless I couldn't go to bed, and I wrote letters and read until quite late."

"What were you reading, Anne?"

"I was looking through a book about rose growing. The gardener had been asking me about some new varieties he had just bought. I'm interested in such things, and the book was well written. But I never want to see it again,— or a rose either."

There was a look of horror in her eyes, and I felt that the rose-book brought back the scenes of that dreadful night so poignantly that she could scarcely bear it.

I changed the subject, and persistently led her mind away from the scene of the tragedy.

"You always do me so much good, Raymond," Anne said, gratefully, as at last we started back to the house; "you always know just what to say to me. You're a real comfort."

"You need and deserve comfort, Anne," I said, gently, "and I think you know you may always depend upon me to give you all I can. And, Anne, if you ever want more of me,—if you want real assistance,—or if you want to confide in me,—you will do so, won't you?"

She turned to me with a startled look. "Why what do you mean?" she asked, and her voice quivered, and she almost gasped for breath.

I looked her straight in the eyes. "I don't mean anything," I said, "except that I am your friend through any circumstance that may come to you. In any trouble or danger,—count on me."

"Even if I have been wicked?" said Anne, in a whisper.

"Yes, even then," but a pang shot through my heart, not so much because of the words she said, as the look of horror and despair that came into her eyes.

The days went by slowly. On Monday the funeral was held, and with appropriate obsequies the body of David Van Wyck was buried. The house guests had all chosen to remain at Buttonwood Terrace, in response to Anne's urgent invitation that we should do so. She seemed to have a dread of being left alone with her step-children, and it became more and more evident that matters were far from harmonious between her and David Van Wyck's son and daughter.

The day after the funeral I had a long talk with Mr. Markham.

"There is no doubt in my mind," he declared, "that Mrs. Van Wyck is the guilty party. We never can fasten the crime upon her, for it cannot be explained how she left the room locked up. But it must be that she did do so in some clever way."

"But there isn't any such way," I objected. "If it were the mere turning of a key, it might be done from the other side, but heavy bolts cannot be shot into their sockets except by a person on the inside of the room. And again, waiving the mystery of the locked room, we are as well justified in suspecting Morland or Barbara as Anne."

"That is true," agreed Markham. "But the stiletto was found in her room, and her maid is missing, and then there is that mysterious letter. That mystery must be sifted out. To my mind it would be better to put the question plainly to Mrs. Van Wyck and ask her what it means."

"I wish you'd try some other way first," I said. "What's the use of being a detective, if you can't trace a letter to its source without asking anybody. Why, if Fleming Stone saw that letter he'd soon tell you who wrote it and what it all meant."

Mr. Markham didn't like this speech, and I didn't blame him. I daresay I ought not to have said it. But he had so little of what is known as the detective method that I couldn't help speaking my mind. "Well, I'll tell you one thing I think about it," he said, "that is, whoever wrote that letter to Mrs. Van Wyck, was certainly her accomplice. Now who could that be, but that valet, Carstairs? He has acted queer from the beginning, and I'm going to hunt him up and make him tell all he knows."

"Carstairs!" I exclaimed in amazement. "You don't think Mrs. Van Wyck would stoop to receiving letters from a servant!"

"If Mrs. Van Wyck has stooped to crime, or participation in crime, she cannot be very particular about her associates."

"But she hasn't stooped to crime! Good heavens, man, don't condemn her unheard!" But even as I spoke, I remembered that Anne had asked me if I would stand by her even if she were wicked! And I had said I would. Yes, and I would, too, even if she were convicted of the worst crime in the calendar!

I don't know whether it was because of my reference to Stone or not, but Markham seemed to acquire new energy. He announced with great determination that he was going to find out about that letter, whatever method he might have to pursue.

And it was partly to divert his sudden energy from this subject, that I proposed again that we should make search for Jeannette.

"Strange about Jeannette," I observed. "Suppose we set out to trace her. That would be at least a step in the right direction."

"There have been very few steps taken in any direction," said the detective moodily. "My own movements are hampered by orders from the family. Of course there's no one to say what I shall do, except Mrs. Van Wyck and her two step-children. And every direction in which I wish to investigate is forbidden by one or another of those three. Sometimes I think they are all in connivance, and their inharmonious attitude toward one another is a mere bluff."

This was a new idea to me, and I pondered it. But I couldn't think it a true theory, and said so.

"Maybe not, maybe not," said Markham; "but they do act mighty queer. Miss Barbara, for instance, begged me if I found any clues which might incriminate her brother, to suppress them and tell nobody."

"Did she really suppose that you would do that?" I asked.

"Yes, she was very much in earnest. But I haven't found anything that points to Morland definitely. If I did, I'd show it up fast enough."

"I should hope so," I returned emphatically.

"I'd far rather suspect Morland of his father's death than Mrs. Van Wyck."

"Yes, so should I. But it's a mystery, whichever way one turns. I can't seem to make any start. But, as you say, Mr. Sturgis, it would be a good idea to hunt for that maid."

It proved not to be a difficult matter to find Jeannette, for we soon discovered that she had gone to stay with her sister in a neighboring village. I couldn't help thinking that Anne had known all along where the girl was, for she seemed rather annoyed than otherwise that we had made the discovery. At any rate, Jeannette was brought home, and closely questioned by Mr. Markham and myself.

And the result of the questioning was to eliminate entirely the stiletto as incriminating evidence. Jeannette explained that she had used that stiletto to dig a refractory cork out of a bottle of bronze shoe-dressing. The bronze had given the metal a reddish stain, which she could not remove, and she had hidden it, lest she be scolded for having used the dainty implement for such a purpose. Markham was frankly disappointed. I can't think he wanted to prove Anne guilty, but his pride was hurt at having his cleverness in finding the stiletto of no avail.

"But," I said to Jeannette, "why did you run away?"

"I didn't run away," she said. "I merely went to visit my sister."

"But you took a strange time to do that, when your mistress was in such trouble and sorrow."

"I thought I'd better go," responded Jeannette; and Markham jumped at this admission.

"Why did you think it better to go?" he demanded.

But Jeannette turned pale and looked very much frightened. "I didn't have any reason," she said, beginning to cry. "I just—I just thought I'd go." We tried every possible way to learn more from her, but without success. She became hysterical and stupid by turns, and finally refused to answer our questions. Markham declared that this attitude on Jeannette's part was strongly against Anne, but this I would not believe.

Finally I said, "Jeannette, the reason you refuse to talk is because you're afraid of Carstairs. Now I'll tell you, it will be better in the long run, if you make a clean breast of this matter and tell us all you know."

And then between her hysterical sobs Jeannette managed to stammer out that Carstairs had said he would kill her if she told.

Certainly she was weak-minded, and I thought the best thing was to scare her a little.

"Nonsense, Jeannette," I said; "of course Carstairs won't kill you. Don't be so foolish. But you may get into very serious trouble if you don't tell this thing that you're keeping back. How would you like to go to prison for withholding evidence?"

The girl shivered at the thought, and a little more of this sort of persuasion soon brought her to the point of saying that she would tell all she knew, but that she knew nothing of importance.

"We will judge of the importance," I said; "and what we want from you is a full account of anything you know concerning last Friday night. In the first place, were you at that ball in the village?"

"No, sir." The answer, though in low tones, was positive.

"Was Carstairs at that ball?"

"No, sir."

"Where were you both?"

It seemed almost as if the girl were hypnotized by my question, for she spoke like one in a trance. Nevertheless her answers bore the stamp of truth and it seemed impossible to doubt that she was telling a straight story.

In the same low steady voice Jeannette went on: "We both went for a ride in Mr. Van Wyck's new car. This was forbidden, of course, but Carstairs said his master would never find it out."

"You went then, on what is called a 'joy ride'?"

"I suppose so."

"And what time did you get home?"

"About midnight."

"Then it was Carstairs that Miss Fordyce saw sneaking into the grounds?"

"I don't know, sir, but Ranney saw us and Carstairs made him promise not to tell."

"At last we're getting at something definite," said Mr. Markham, fairly rubbing his hands with pleasure at these new developments. He then took up the work of questioning himself.

"You came into the house about twelve o'clock that night?"

"Yes, sir."

"And then what did you do?"

"I stopped in the servants' dining-room, sir, and in a few minutes, Carstairs came in there after putting away the car. He said nobody had seen us except Ranney and he wouldn't tell. Then he told me I'd better go and see if Mrs. Van Wyck wanted me. So I started for Mrs. Van Wyck's room, but before I reached it, I saw her coming out of the study."

"Coming out of the study! Be careful what you're saying, girl! Are you sure of this?"

"Of course I'm sure. Mrs. Van Wyck had on one of her boudoir gowns, and she was just coming through the study door into the corridor as I saw her. I asked her if she wanted me to help her undress."

"And what did she say?" The detective was almost breathless now in his excitement.

"She said, ' No, no! for heaven's sake go away!'"

"Why did she speak like that?"

"I don't know, sir. She was greatly excited, and her eyes were blazing like stars. She was clutching her hands and she looked almost distracted."

"Jeannette," I said, very sternly, "you're telling the truth?"

"Only the truth, sir. I was frightened at Mrs. Van Wyck's appearance, but as she said she didn't want me, I went straight back to the servants' diningroom. I found Carstairs there, and he looked frightened and white, too. I was all upset, sir, at these queer actions, and I said good-night to Carstairs and went right up to my room."

"At what time was all this?" asked Mr. Markham.

"When I reached my bedroom it was half-past twelve."

Mr. Markham looked at the girl thoughtfully. "I believe your story," he said, "but you will have to tell it again under oath. And in the meantime I forbid you to mention a word of this to anyone. Do you understand? I forbid you!"

"Yes, sir."

"You ought to have been here and given this evidence at the inquest. Why did you go away just then? You may as well own up."

Jeannette hesitated only a moment, and then she said simply, "Mrs. Carstairs advised me to go."

"Mrs. Carstairs! Why did she do that?"

"I don't know, sir. She said for me to go to my sister's for a day or two and make a little visit."

"That is all for the present, Jeannette," said Mr. Markham. You may go now, but remember you are not to say a word about all this to anyone."

"I will remember, sir," said Jeannette, and she went away.

CHAPTER 16: TELLTALE TYPEWRITING

AFTER the girl had gone Mr. Markham looked at me significantly. "We certainly have material to work on now," he said. "What do you make of it all, Mr. Sturgis?"

"I can't make anything of it," I replied. "It has all come upon me so suddenly it makes my head whirl. Of course I see, as you do, that this girl's story is pretty strong evidence against Mrs. Van Wyck, but I, for one, am not willing to take the unsupported evidence of a hysterical and weakminded servant."

"But how can you doubt it? The girl would never have made up all that story. You don't question, do you, the fact that she saw Mrs. Van Wyck coming from the study, soon after midnight? Then how do you explain Mrs. Van Wyck's presence there, after the men of the committee had gone home and the secretary had also? How do you explain the fact that she was wringing her hands, in a state of great excitement, and even spoke sharply as she declined the services of the maid?"

"I don't explain these facts, if they are facts. But as I said, I'm not prepared to believe this story implicitly. I do believe those two went on a 'joy ride' and they came home so frightened lest their misdemeanor should be discovered, that they haven't a very clear recollection of what happened. At least the girl hasn't, and as you may remember the valet was decidedly nervous and uncertain of his facts when he gave his own testimony. Besides telling an up and down lie as to his whereabouts that evening."

"That's all so," said the detective, musingly.

"They're both servants. They had both been doing wrong and were both fearful of discovery. But all that would not cause them to invent this story of the maid's about seeing Mrs. Van Wyck coming from the study. Now if, as I think, Carstairs was mixed up in the matter, may it not be that it was because she feared for her son's safety that Mrs. Carstairs sent the girl, Jeannette, away?"

I pondered on this. I knew how Mrs. Carstairs idolized her son. I knew she had been out early that next morning endeavoring to obliterate the wheel tracks of the new car, which might tell the tale of his wrong-doing. And knowing Jeannette's hysterical nature, the housekeeper might very easily have felt afraid that the maid's evidence would lead to suspicion of her son and so she sent the girl away. It all looked plausible, so plausible that my fears for Anne grew deeper, and the future looked very blade indeed.

"If my theory is right," Mark ham went on, "that there is collusion between Mrs. Van Wyck and the valet, I think the best plan is to question him. I think if sufficiently frightened, he will tell the truth. And now he has no fear of punishment for his stolen ride, he will probably make up some other story and I may yet catch him tripping. But I think this, Mr. Sturgis, I think it is high time we gave all this information to the other members of the family. My way would be, to go straight to Mrs. Van Wyck with the whole story; but if not that, I think at least Miss Van Wyck and her brother, should be told all of this. They are practically my employers and my report is due to them."

"Give me a little more time," I begged. "Wait till to-night, won't you? If I could prove this girl's story false, how much better not to have insulted Mrs. Van Wyck with a recital of it."

"It seems to me, Mr. Sturgis, that you're assuming a great deal of responsibility in the matter."

"But who else is there to take the helm? Morland Van Wyck is not one to deal with such things, and the ladies could not be expected to do so."

And then as it was tea-time, we joined the others in the music-room.

Of course, since the tragedy, tea had not been served in the study, and the beautiful music-room made an attractive setting for the dainty function. As was to be expected, there was an air of constraint over us all; and instead of general conversation, we broke up into small groups and conversed in low tones.

As was not unusual, Morland and Barbara were disagreeing on some subject. A few words in their raised voices proved that they were discussing the lost pearls.

Somewhat to my surprise, Mr. Lasseter took part in their argument.

"It couldn't have been a burglar," Lasseter was saying, "because he would never have stolen that Deed of Gift. That theft proves positively the work of some one interested in behalf of the family. And so Morland, as you can't believe there were two thieves, I think you must agree that the criminal was some interested party."

"Are you accusing me?" burst out Morland. "Do you perhaps think that I raised my hand against my own father?"

"I accuse nobody," said Lasseter, "but I think we ought to make more progress toward discovering the criminal. I cast no implication on Mr. Markham's work, but I do say that it is a most mysterious case, and perhaps Mr. Markham himself would like it better if he could have some one of his own profession to consult with."

I was astonished that the secretary should so assert himself, as to make this suggestion, for as a rule, he was rather reticent and non-committal. Moreover, I knew that the one he had in mind was Fleming Stone.

Morland opposed this idea and said rather angrily that there was no use throwing away any more money on detectives, when the one we had didn't amount to anything.

I felt decidedly uncomfortable at this, for, if I had not held him back, Mr. Markham would have told the family of his recent discoveries. The glance that the detective shot at me expressed this thought, and I partly made up my mind that I would tell him to go ahead in his own way. I left the party and walked out on the terrace alone. It seemed as if I must do something desperate. I had promised Markham that if I discovered nothing about that letter by evening, I would consent to his making the story public. I had vague thoughts of going straight to Anne with it as it would be easier for her to hear about it from me alone than from the detective in the presence of others.

But I couldn't bring myself to do this.

I tried to think what Fleming Stone would do if he had that letter to puzzle over. And I thought at once, that he would examine it to the minutest detail, even under a lens.

At any rate, it was something to try; so I asked Markham for the letter and he gave it to me unnoticed by anyone else. Remembering that there was a magnifying-glass in the study, I took the letter in there.

Although the scene of the crime the great room was so beautiful that it gave no sense of horror. I crossed the soft Turkish rug to the desk that had been Mr. Van Wyck's. The lens was there, and I read the letter through it. The magnifying of it told me nothing, but as I reread the terrible lines, I could not believe they were written to Anne in good faith. I believed the letter a forgery of some sort, and I determined to find out.

I had heard Stone say that typewriting was almost as individual as pen-writing. That no two typewriters produced the same script and, indeed, no two operators wrote alike, even on the same machine. And so I set to work to note any peculiarities I might find in the words or letters.

At the very outset I made a discovery. This was that the typewriting on the envelope and inside the letter were not the same! There could be no doubt that they were not done on the same machine. The ink was the same color, the letters about the same size; but the conformation, though similar, was not identical. I wondered what this could mean, for surely the paper and envelope belonged to each other, and why would anyone write a letter on one typewriter and address it on another?

Spurred on by this discovery I scrutinized still more carefully, and found that in the message the capital " T " was imperfect. A tiny corner of one of its arms failed to print. This was a small thing, but it was a certain thing. The " T " on the envelope was perfectly clear and distinct.

I could find no other discrepancies of this kind, but I was positive that the fact of two typewriters having been used, proved chicanery of some sort. Then, again, I thought perhaps a letter might print clearly at one time and not at another. As an experiment I went to the typewriter which stood on a side table in the study, and hastily wrote a few lines. I did not copy the letter or the address, but wrote a familiar quotation of some sort, followed by a whole string of letters at random.

Removing my paper I could scarcely believe my eyes as I looked at it. The capital "T," in every instance, was imperfect in precisely the same manner as the one in Anne's letter. There was no doubt of this. I wrote a whole line of " T's " and it was impossible to make the key print it clearly. I made further examination of my slip of paper, and found that every letter had the same peculiarities as the corresponding letters in the mysterious note. They were infinitesimal peculiarities, but they were indubitable. Whoever wrote that letter to Anne Van Wyck, wrote it on that machine that was now before me and no other! But the envelope was just as certainly not addressed on that particular typewriter! Now what did this mean, I asked myself. And it was a long time before I could grasp the answer, but it finally came to me in a flash of inspiration! As I had suspected, the letter was a forgery; it had been written on David Van Wyck's typewriter by some one who could get access to it either secretly or openly; and it had been placed in an envelope which had contained another letter already received and opened by Anne! A plan of diabolical ingenuity! of wicked cleverness!

I still sat by the machine, looking at the letter, when the faintest sound caught my ear and I glanced up to see Mrs. Carstairs gliding toward me. She was just at my elbow and was actually about to snatch the letter from my hand. Indeed her fingers almost touched it.

I stared at her, and said quietly, "What does this mean? Do you want this letter?"

"Oh," she said, and her face showed a cajoling smile; "I beg your pardon, I do indeed! I thought you were copying it."

"And what if I was?" I said, partly angry and wholly mystified.

"Don't be angry," and her alluring face wore a coaxing expression; "please give me the letter."

"Give you the letter! Why should I do that?"

She went so far as to lay her hand on my shoulder, and said softly: "I know I did wrong. I ought never to have read it, but having read it, I ought never to have shown it."

"I quite agree to all that, Mrs. Carstairs, but having given it into the hands of the detective, you may not take it back."

I spoke sternly, even more sharply than I meant to, for I was afraid the woman's wiles would get that letter away from me against my will.

Then she said: "Mr. Sturgis,—please,"—and no words can express the persuasive power of her look and voice,— " won't you please do this, then? Copy the letter, if you want to, but give back the original."

"Why?" I asked, eying her closely.

"Because I'm sure I did wrong to take it; and I want to restore it to Mrs. Van Wyck."

Now of course I had no intention of granting her request, and I'm almost sure I should not have done so, but I may as well admit that I was greatly relieved that Markham entered the room at that moment.

She turned to the detective with a pretty pout that was almost girlish. "Can't I have the letter, Mr. Markham?" she begged.

"Have the letter? Certainly not, madam! It is without a doubt a most important clue."

Surely Mr. Markham was proof against her blandishments, and she realized that there was no hope to regain possession of the letter.

"Oh, well," she said, lightly, "it's of no consequence. If it gets Mrs. Van Wyck into trouble, I'm sure *I* can't help it. I've done all I could to retrieve what was perhaps a mistake on my part. Now, she may take the consequences!"

Mrs. Carstairs glided from the room, seeming not at all disappointed, but actually triumphant. "I give her up," I said to Markham; "do you think she really wanted that letter back for Mrs. Van Wyck's benefit, or for some other reason?"

"I can't think of any other reason; I think she found the letter, and brought it to me from a sense of duty. Then I think she felt sorry that she had given such awful evidence against Mrs. Van Wyck and wanted to retract it."

"Markham," I said, abruptly, "that letter was written in this room, on David Van Wyck's own typewriter."

"Did he write it himself?" Markham seemed absolutely unable to sense my statement, which must have accounted for his absurd remark.

"Of course he didn't write it himself!" I said impatiently; "but somebody wrote it, on this very typewriter. Here, I'll prove it to you."

I showed Markham how I had discovered the fact, and proved to him beyond any doubt, that whoever wrote the letter, it had certainly been done on that machine.

There were a dozen little peculiarities that made it impossible to be otherwise.

"What's the answer?" said Markham, looking absolutely blank.

"I don't know. If the letter is in good faith, it means an accomplice in the crime. But if the letter is a fake, which I think it is, it is written by somebody who wants to throw suspicion on Mrs. Van Wyck. As you see, the address on the envelope is not done on this machine. That envelope, whatever its contents may have been, was mailed and delivered from the village post-office last Friday. Now, Mr. Detective, solve the problem."

"To begin with," said Markham, thoughtfully, "if it was done in this room it must have been done by some member of the family."

"Or some servant or some guest," I supplemented him.

"No guest would do it. No servant would have opportunity to do it; and beside, the diction and construction of the note is not that of an uneducated person."

"Well, go over all the members of the household. Of course it was neither David Van Wyck or his wife. Equally of course, it was neither of his children."

"Why not?"

"Good heavens, man, because that's impossible! Do you suppose either Morland or Barbara connived with Anne Van Wyck to kill her husband? Absurd!"

"But if the letter is merely a blind?"

"Well, even so. Neither of those two young people would do this thing to incriminate their stepmother. Morland is more than half in love with her; and I refuse to suspect Barbara. Go through with the house guests. Archer and myself would move Heaven and earth to shield Mrs. Van Wyck, rather than to bring trouble to her. Mrs. Stelton and Miss Fordyce are simply out of the question. How about the two Carstairs?"

"That woman was certainly not in league with Mrs. Van Wyck for any purpose; but I've already told you that I'm quite ready to suspect her son."

"The valet?"

"Yes; if he were in league with Mrs. Van Wyck, —now keep your temper,—if they were accomplices in this matter, would that not fulfil every condition of this letter? He wrote it to her, we'll say, having access to this room at certain times. Then, unable to give it to her himself, he mails it in the morning, in most ordinary fashion, and she gets it in the afternoon."

I nearly throttled the man. "Do you mean then, that after this advice, Mrs. Van Wyck murdered her husband, being assured of the aid and protection of his valet?"

"That's what I mean,"—and Mr. Markham gave me a quiet but meaningful glance, that quelled my anger as no protestations could have done. I had to stop and think. I had known Anne only a few days,—really; how could I tell of what she might be capable? And I could never forget her assertion that she was capable of crime! But to be leagued with a servant,—against her husband,—it was unthinkable! At last I burst out:

"I won't believe it! I won't listen to it. And you've left out one member of this household! What about that precious secretary? He has access to this room at all times. We know almost nothing about him. Why may it not be he who connived with his employer's wife?"

"In the first place," said Markham, "he is devoted to Miss Barbara. I fancy they're engaged. But it may be,—it may be that he is really in love with Mrs. Van Wyck—I tell you, Mr. Sturgis, more crimes are committed for love than for money!"

"Then what about Carstairs?" I countered. If he had any motive it must have been the money that he knew he would get at his master's death. He could have had no other reason. You don't suppose, do you, that he lifted his eyes to his master's wife?"

"I don't suppose anything!" and Markham, passed his hand wearily over his brow. "I have nothing to do with supposition. I must find tangible clues and positive evidence. I have nothing but this letter to work upon. I am glad of your aid, Mr. Sturgis, for I confess I find it a most baffling case. But unless you are willing to look at the matter from all sides, you can be of little assistance to me."

"I will help you all I can, Mr. Markham, but I make this condition. Don't tell of this letter quite yet. It is, as you say, a tangible clue, and I think we ought to learn something from it. But if you exploit it, you will only have panic as a result!"

After a little further persuasion, Markham agreed to say nothing of the letter just at present He said we would both try our best to discover the truth from it; and I curbed ray anger and indignation at his base suspicions, because I really wanted to aid him.

As a matter of fact, I was the only one who aided Markham in his investigations, or who even seemed interested in their results. Sometimes Anne would talk with us, but she was so contradictory and made such untenable suggestions, that I could scarcely find out what her desires or intentions were. Barbara had taken the stand that she wished investigation stopped. I could not learn her reasons for this, but I began to think it was because she feared what might be learned from them. Morland, I had reason to think, knew more about the matter than he was willing to tell. Whether he was guilty himself, or whether he knew the guilty person, I could not decide, but I was sure one or the other must be the case.

I talked it all over with Condron Archer. He seemed to me to look at the matter very sensibly. "On the face of things," he said, "you must admit, Sturgis, that it looks as if one of the three Van Wycks must be implicated. So it appears to me that if we can throw suspicion elsewhere, it would save the Van Wyck family."

"And you would advise that?" I said in surprise. "You would willingly cast suspicion on an innocent person in order to shield one of the Van Wycks?"

He looked straight at me. "Wouldn't you," he asked, "if it were Anne who was in danger?"

"I don't know," I said slowly.

"You ought to know," he declared. "Look here, Sturgis, what is the use of denying the truth to each other? You are in love with Anne Van Wyck, and so am I. I don't for a moment believe that she killed her husband, but if she did, I'd rather not know it. Now, should we not do anything in our power to divert suspicion from her? I wouldn't accuse or convict an innocent man, but if by directing suspicion away from Anne we can save her, let us do so. And then afterward, let the better man win her."

I had little doubt from Archer's assured air that he felt certain he himself would prove the better man, but I was not so sure of this. However, for the moment I must consider his proposition. I told him that I would certainly do all in my power to shield Anne, but it was because I believed her innocent, and not because I feared she was guilty. But he merely shrugged his shoulders at this, and gave me the impression, without saying so, that he thought me insincere.

CHAPTER 17: THE SEARCH FOR THE PEARLS

IT was a strange sort of gloom that hung over us all at Buttonwood Terrace. It was not exactly sorrow; indeed, there was little evidence of real grief for David Van Wyck. His children, if they mourned for him, did not do so openly; while his wife seemed stunned rather than saddened. I could not understand Anne. She seemed to pass rapidly from one strange mood to another. Now she would be most anxious to discover the murderer and avenge the crime, and again she would beg of us to discontinue all investigation.

Archer watched her closely. It seemed to me he suspected her, and wanted to make sure, but he wanted no one else to suspect her.

David Van Wyck had died on Friday night, and the funeral had occurred on Monday. It was now Wednesday, and the inquest would be resumed in a few days. But to my way of thinking, we had little if any more evidence to go on. Jeannette had explained the stiletto, but who knew if she had told the truth? Doubtless she would lie to shield Anne, for she was devoted to her mistress, and the reasons she had given for going away seemed to me far from plausible. Moreover, Anne had expressed no surprise or annoyance at the girl's absence, which I was forced to admit looked as if the mistress had thoroughly understood it.

It was on Wednesday morning that I was strolling along the terraces, thinking deeply, when I became aware of voices below me. I glanced down a winding, rustic stairway and saw Anne and Condron Archer. He seemed to be pleading with her, and she looked disturbed and a trifle defiant. I turned away, having no desire to be an eaves-dropper, but as I turned, Archer's voice rose in emphatic declaration, and I couldn't help hearing his words.

He said, "Anne, I know you took the pearls. Now, promise you will marry me some day, and so give me the right to shield and protect you in this trial."

The shock of his speech was so great that I involuntarily paused for an instant, and I heard Anne say, "I deny that I took the pearls. If you think I did, you may search for them. I defy you to find them!"

I hurried away from the spot, suddenly realizing that I was listening; and I am quite willing to confess to a strong desire to listen longer. But this I would not do, partly because my sense of honor forbade it, and also because Anne was the woman I loved, and I would not listen to a word of hers that was not meant for my ears.

A moment later I met Barbara and Morland, and they too were talking of the missing pearls.

"Don't you think, Mr. Sturgis," said Barbara, "that we ought to make a thorough and systematic search of the house for those pearls before we consider putting the matter in the hands of the police? They represent a fortune in themselves, and I am sure that my father hid them after he had lost control of his mind. It seems to me, then, that they must be somewhere in the study, and we ought to be able to find them."

"It can certainly do no harm to search," I responded, non-committally, "but I supposed you had already done so."

"We have, in a general way," said Morland; "but Barb means to try to find some secret cupboard or sliding panel hitherto unknown."

"I'm with you," I said. "Let's begin at once. Anything is better than doing nothing; and I do think, Morland, that you're making very little effort to solve the whole mystery. If I were you, I should call in Fleming Stone."

"No!" cried Barbara, so sharply that I was surprised. "There is no occasion for such a thing," she went on. "Father killed himself. His mind gave way at the last, and he was not responsible. Also, he hid the pearls, and we can find them. Come on and let us begin the search. Here are Anne and Mr. Archer—they will help, I'm sure."

After listening to Barbara's request, both Anne and Archer heartily agreed to help in a thorough search. We went at once to the study. Markham and Lasseter were already there, and we all went to work with a will. I think I'm safe in saying that no room was ever searched more carefully than the Van Wyck study was that day. We divided it into sections, and each of us searched every section. Mrs. Stelton and Beth Fordyce joined us later, and every possible hiding-place was ransacked. Nor was it an easy task. There were many cupboards and desks and odd pieces of furniture with secret drawers. And besides, there were many possible hiding-places in the massive and intricate ornamentations. The enormous carved fireplace seemed to mock at us with its possibilities. The carved wainscot and stuccoed wall-panels all showed interstices which, though in some cases thick with the dust of time, were large enough to hold a pearl necklace. Anne was perhaps the most energetic of all the searchers. She ran up the spiral staircase to the musicians' gallery and called for some one to come and help her. "For," said she, "this carved railing is simply full of places where anything could be hidden!"

As I looked up and saw Anne leaning forward with both hands on the balcony rail, I thought I had never seen a more beautiful picture. Whether it was the mere exertion of the search, or the result of some secret knowledge of her own, her cheeks were flushed and her eyes were bright with an unnatural excitement.

I ran up the iron staircase, myself, in response to her invitation, and as no one followed us, I drew her back into the shadow of the curtain draperies, and, clasping both her hands in mine, I said earnestly, "Anne, you don't know where the pearls are, do you?"

Her hands turned cold in mine, and the color died from her cheeks. "How dare you!" she whispered. "What do you mean? What are you implying?"

"Nothing." And, unable to control myself, I clasped her in my arms. But only for a moment, and then, my senses returning, I released her, and said calmly, "I mean nothing, Anne. Forgive me, I lost my head for a moment. But you must know what I shall some day tell you, that I love you, and I shall yet win you. Hush, don't answer me now! But just remember that I have utter faith in you, and because of that faith I shall probe this whole mystery to its furthest depths. I shall learn the truth, the whole truth, and then, Anne, when it is the proper time, I shall claim you, and you will give yourself to me!" I have wondered since how I had the courage to make these statements, for Anne gave me no encouragement. She merely stared at me, her dark eyes seeming to burn like coals of fire in her white face. But as I finished she gave a little despairing sob, and said pitifully, "Oh, Raymond, you don't know, you don't know!"

And then Beth Fordyce came up to the gallery, and both Anne and I controlled ourselves sufficiently to speak casually, as we all continued our search. The gallery was six feet wide and extended across the whole end of the room, except for a space of about four feet from either side-wall. It rested on six enormously heavy brackets, and its railing, about three feet high, was also heavy and elaborate. Miss Fordyce looked over the railing in despair. "We never can look into every cranny of those brackets," she said.

"We can do it by ladders from below," I returned; "but I will say that I never saw any room so marvellously well provided with hiding-places." Anne stood at the end of the gallery, but not the staircase end, and looked at the great cartouche that formed the corner of the cornice, but which was so massive that its lower end was on a level with the gallery.

"I can't reach it," she said, stretching out her hand toward its plaster scroll-work; "but the pearls could be in any of those gilded crevices."

"And there are four of those great ornaments in the room," said I, looking hopelessly around at the cornice. "But if Mr. Van Wyck secreted his jewels in one of them, he must have had a long ladder; and where is the ladder?"

"He might have had a rope-ladder," suggested Mrs. Stelton, looking self-conscious, as if she had voiced a brilliant idea.

"But, even so, it must be somewhere, and we have found nothing of the sort," I said.

Well, the search lasted all the morning, without the least result. And, to my surprise, after luncheon Mr. Markham proposed that we should search the other rooms of the house. "I have my own reasons for this," he declared, and as this was the first time I had known him to assume the mysterious air which is part of the stock in trade of every self-respecting detective, I began to hope his reasons might be sound ones.

No one was enthusiastic about a further search, but all agreed to it, except Anne. She declared that the privacy of her own rooms should not be invaded, and she refused to allow search to be made in them. At this, I saw Archer look at her intently; I saw Anne flush with anger and dismay; and I saw Mr. Markham alertly observing both.

"It is a mere matter of form, Mrs. Van Wyck," he said; "but I must insist upon it. And of course you must see that to close your rooms to our search would look--" He hesitated; even he could not voice the implication he was about to make, in the face of Anne's scorn.

"That will do," she said coldly, and at once led the way to her own apartments.

Her bedroom, dressing-room, and bathroom were subjected to a search, but, on the part of most of us, it was perfunctory and superficial. Except the detective, not

one of us was willing to open the cupboards, boxes, or
bureau-drawers. But Mr. Markham darted here and
there, opening drawers, boxes, and baskets, one after
another. I chanced to be sitting by a table on which was a
gilded Florentine chest, which was locked. Markham
demanded the key, and Anne gave it to him. But the
chest was entirely empty, save for several old
photographs carelessly flung in. Disappointed, the
detective stared thoughtfully about the room.

"You must understand, Mrs. Van Wyck," he said
smoothly, "that we have no suspicion, but at the same
time we must make this search a thorough one. And I
think we have examined everything except the book-
shelves. I must ask now that the books be taken down."

The book-shelves, which were built against the wall,
covered nearly all one side of the room. At Mr.
Markham's orders, the books were taken down, three or
four at a time, and returned to their places; but, although
there was plenty of space behind them, no pearls were
discovered.

"Shall we open each book?" inquired Mr. Archer
sarcastically.

"No," said the detective shortly. "Pearls could not be
placed in a book, but they could easily be hidden behind
them, and I must do my duty." The others had helped
with the book-shelf performance, but I had stayed near
Anne. She was trembling like a leaf. If she had hidden
the pearls behind the books, and feared their discovery,
she could not have been more nervously agitated. I
noticed, too, that Archer was watching her closely, even
while he was busily engaged in taking down and putting
back the volumes.

In an effort to distract Anne's attention, and perhaps
to calm her unrest, I said, "How did you like the vase I
brought you?" and I glanced at it where it stood on a
small side table.

"It is beautiful!" she said, and she thanked me with
her eyes. "I have never seen a more exquisite piece of

Venetian glass. But so very fragile! I would not let any one but myself touch it to unpack it; and even then I was afraid it would break while I was disengaging it from its wrappings. I was frightened, Raymond, lest Mr. Van Wyck should see it. He was so absurdly jealous that it would have made him very angry. But now it doesn't matter." Her lip quivered, and a strange look came into her eyes, but I was positive it was not regret that she no longer had to endure her husband's jealousy. At last Markham declared himself satisfied that the pearls were not in Anne's apartments, and, followed by his assistants, he went to search David Van Wyck's rooms. And from there the search continued all over the rest of the rooms; and it was well on toward sundown before he was ready to declare himself satisfied that the pearls were not hidden in any part of the house.

"And so," said Mr. Markham, with an air of finality, "we may be sure that Mr. Van Wyck did not hide the pearls, nor are they in the possession of any member of this household. This, I think, proves that the robbery was committed by an intruder, who also killed Mr. Van Wyck. The mystery of how the burglar entered, and what weapon he used, will, I fear, never be solved."

"And the missing deed?" asked Archer. "That is another mystery that seems inexplicable. Of course the fortune now remains in possession of the family, and will be disposed of according to the terms of Mr. Van Wyck's will."

The will, as everybody knew, left David Van Wyck's three heirs each in possession of one-third of his fortune. The pearls were not mentioned in the will, although Anne claimed he had verbally given them to her. Both Barbara and Morland disputed her ownership of them, but as the pearls were gone, it made little difference whose they were.

"I can't help thinking, Mr. Markham," I said, "that we have all reached the end of our ingenuity. But I also think that the problem ought not to be given up, and that it is now time to call in a more expert investigator. I propose, therefore, that we send for Fleming Stone, and put the matter in his hands."

"Oh, that wonderful Mr. Stone!" exclaimed Mrs. Stelton, clapping her hands in her foolish way.

"Send for him, do! He can tell us everything!"

"I, for one, do not wish him sent for," said Anne, in a most positive manner.

"Nor I," said Barbara, for once agreeing with her step-mother.

"I don't think we need him," said Morland thoughtfully. "What could he find out more than I have?"

"We haven't found out anything," I retorted. "And he would explain everything in a short time."

"Is he, then, omniscient?" said Mr. Markham, with a decided sneer.

"He is very nearly so in matters of detective work," I returned gravely. "If Mrs. Van Wyck does not wish to employ him, I will do so myself; as I am quite willing to admit that I have a strong desire to solve the mysteries of David Van Wyck's death and of the stolen jewels and missing deed." We discussed at some length the question of sending for Fleming Stone, but so strong was the opposition of the Van Wycks, of the detective, and of Condron Archer, that I forbore to insist, and the matter was left unsettled.

But later I discussed it alone with Archer.

"Don't do it," he said to me earnestly. "Don't you see that to get Stone here might implicate Anne?"

"Why," said I, in surprise, "my motive in getting him would be to prove Anne's innocence!"

"Then, if you want to prove Anne Van Wyck innocent, or even to continue to think her so, don't send for Stone;" and with these words, Archer turned on his heel and left me.

I went to the study, hoping to find Morland there, and to persuade him to agree to my views. But there was no one in the study except the secretary.

"Mr. Lasseter," I said, "as man to man, won't you explain to me why you and Morland persist in those conflicting stories?"

"My story is the true one," said Lasseter, looking me squarely in the eye. "When I left the room that night, Morland sat here"—indicating a large carved seat near the fireplace—"and Mr. Van Wyck was at his desk. It all occurred as I related at the inquest. And, Mr. Sturgis, I will tell you what I have not told any one else. After going out of the door, I went around the study and half way down the front path to the road. Then, on an impulse which I cannot explain, I turned back and went and looked in at the study window—not the door, but the window at the farther end. And I distinctly saw Morland bending over his father's desk. Of course at that time I had no thought of tragedy, and I hoped that father and son would make up their quarrel then and there. I merely glanced in, and, turning away again, went straight home."

"Why didn't you tell of this at the inquest?"

"Because, though it would, in a way, prove my story, in the face of the tragedy I feared it might make things look black for Morland."

"You don't suspect him of—of any wrongdoing!"

"No, I can't. But it is all mysterious, and I agree with you in wishing that we could have the great Fleming Stone look into it."

"Why, I thought you didn't want him!"

"Personally I do; but since Miss Van Wyck is so opposed to the idea, I should rather defer to her wishes than insist upon my own."

"Oh, I see; I didn't understand before."

"Yes," said Lasseter frankly; "although we're not formally engaged, I hope to make Barbara Van Wyck my wife; and so, you see, I cannot endorse a course of action to which she is so definitely opposed."

This was true enough, and I told him so. I couldn't help liking Lasseter, and some things about him which I had thought strange were explained by what he had just told me.

From him I went straight to Morland. "Tell me," I said to him, in a confidential way, "why did you and Lasseter contradict each other at the inquest?"

"I wondered you didn't ask me that long ago," he said, seeming not at all offended. "You see, it is this way. I was sitting on that old bench by the fireplace. But it is in a dark corner, and I was in a shadow; for after the committee left we had turned off some of the lights, and the shaded desk-light and the firelight made pretty much all the illumination there was. I was tired and discouraged with the whole matter, and I left the room quietly, just before twelve, without even saying good-night. Father and Lasseter were talking, and I don't believe they heard me go. So when Lasseter said good-night to me, as he says he did, he really thought I was there; and if Father spoke to me, why, he must have thought so, too."

This was all plausible enough, and the young man's frank manner convinced me of its truth. But there was another point to be cleared up.

"All right, Morland," I said. "That does explain things. You left the room just before midnight, and a moment or two later Lasseter went home, and said good-night to you, thinking you were there. But, a little later still, you returned."

"What!" cried Morland, and he turned fairly livid with rage. "What do you mean, Sturgis?"

"What do you mean by getting so excited over it? You did return, and you were seen."

"By whom?"

"Never mind that now."

Morland looked straight at me. There was fear in his eyes, but there was also a strong ring of truth in his voice as he said,"' Sturgis, if I returned to the study, and if I was seen there, then the one who saw me is the murderer! Send for your Fleming Stone and discover who it may be!"

Without another word, Morland strode away, leaving me completely bewildered by his words.

CHAPTER 18: FLEMING STONE ARRIVES

WHEN I went to my room to dress for dinner, I thought the matter over very definitely, before deciding to send for Stone. It was a somewhat radical move on my part, and I was not sure that I was entirely justified; but I felt that I must clear Anne of any possible breath of suspicion. And as I was unable to do this by myself, I wanted the best possible assistance I could find. And yet everybody was opposed to the coming of the great detective. I felt sure that Barbara didn't want him to come, because she suspected the guilt of either her brother or the secretary. I could see this from the way in which she looked at both men, and from some slight hints she had inadvertently dropped in conversation. And since it seemed to be fairly well proven that Morland Van Wyck and Barclay Lasseter were the last two people known to be with David Van Wyck, then one was, in a way, justified in suspecting one or both of these men. And Barbara, fearful that Fleming Stone's coming would mean disaster to her brother or her lover, naturally protested against it. Condron Archer had said frankly that he didn't want Stone to come, lest he might implicate Anne; and when I remembered Anne's various inexplicable actions, and especially her agitation during the search in her room, I too trembled to think what Fleming Stone's investigations might disclose. Markham, the detective, I knew, didn't want Stone, but that I ascribed to a petty professional jealousy. Of course the two detectives were not to be mentioned on the same day of the week, but Markham, in his ignorance, considered himself quite the peer of Stone.

But, on the other hand, Lasseter, I knew, really wanted Stone, and only refrained from saying so out of consideration for Barbara. This to me was a fair proof of Lasseter's own innocence. And, indeed, no breath of real suspicion had fallen on the secretary, except the general fact that he had had opportunity to steal the pearls, had he been inclined to do so.

But what had brought my inclinations to a positive decision was the fact that Morland had said to send for Fleming Stone. He said it in the heat of passion and under the influence of anger; but he had said it, and I decided to consider that as authority. So I concluded to write at once, before Morland could retract his permission.

I made a rapid toilet, and found I had time enough left before dinner to write my letter.It was not an easy matter, for I was not one of the principals in the case, and I didn't wish to tell Stone of my hopes regarding Anne. But I wrote a straightforward account of everything, and I begged him to come at once. I told him frankly that most of the household were opposed to his coming, but that Morland had sanctioned it, and that if there were ever any question of authority, I would assume all the responsibility of having asked him, and would also be responsible for the financial settlement. As I wrote, my mind became more firmly made up that I was doing right. I could never marry Anne while she was under this cloud, and, even should she refuse to marry me, I must free her from any taint of suspicion regarding her husband's death. Of Archer's hint that Stone's coming might convict Anne of the crime, I resolutely took no notice. If I could believe such a thing of the woman I loved, I would be utterly unworthy of her.

But I wrote nothing of all this to Stone. I told him the simple facts of the case as I knew them; I told him the indications and evidences as I knew them; and I must admit that it did seem a tangle. I felt that we had been either stupid or inefficient in our endeavors to unravel the mystery; for they certainly had led nowhere. All suspicion of any person fell to the ground before the undeniable fact of that sealed room. And all suspicion of suicide fell to the ground in the absence of any weapon. Truly it was a case worthy of Fleming Stone's attention, and I hoped with all my heart he would take it up. With the thought of helping him to understand it all, I wrote him everything we had done. I told of Jeannette's disappearance, of the hidden stiletto, and of her subsequent explanation. I told him of our exhaustive search for the pearls, and I told him, too, though I hated to, how nervous and agitated Anne was when we searched her book-shelves. And then I told him, though I fully realized that all these things pointed in one direction, of the last words David Van Wyck said to his wife as he left the drawing-room. How he had told her he was going to give away the pearls she looked upon as her own, and how he had said, "Now don't you wish I were dead?" I admitted to him that Anne was very strongly opposed to the munificent gift her husband had intended making, but stated also that the disappeance of the deed was quite as favorable to the wishes of the two stepchildren as to those of the wife.

I told Fleming Stone all this, and I told him, too, that I believed Anne Van Wyck innocent; but for this belief I could give no reason.

That letter went off Wednesday night. I sent it to the permanent address in New York which Stone had given me, though of course I had no means of knowing whether he was there or not. But by good fortune he was in New York, and he replied to my letter at once, so that late Thursday afternoon I received his reply.

To my satisfaction, he declared himself willing to undertake the case, and incidentally complimented me on the clearness of my account and the definiteness of my written details. He said he would arrive Friday morning, and he begged me to keep the room from being disturbed any further. "Though, I dare say," he wrote, "that by this time all possible clues are removed or destroyed through ignorance or carelessness. However, lock up the room at once, and let no one enter it until I get there."

This instruction was scarcely necessary, for the study had had few occupants since the tragedy. Everybody avoided the place, and the servants could scarcely be induced to enter it. I knew it had not been swept or dusted since the fatal night, and I hoped that Stone's marvellous powers could find clues where we had seen none. To be sure, we had searched it thoroughly for the pearls, and no one of us had then found anything in the way of evidence. But we were not trained observers, and I had great hopes of Stone's wizardry. After dinner, I walked on the terrace with Anne. I had announced at the dinner-table that I had written for Fleming Stone, and that I had done this with Morland's consent.

I glanced at Morland as I said this, but he made no response beyond a slight affirmative nod. There was a silence after my announcement, and then Mrs. Stelton began to babble, and Beth Fordyce began a rapturous eulogy of Fleming Stone and his work. But the others said nothing, either for or against the coming of the detective.

As we walked on the terrace, I tried to draw Anne out on the subject. But she only said wearily, "It doesn't matter. It would have to come out some time, I suppose. Shall you mind, Raymond, when your friend Stone proves me a criminal—?"

"I don't think he will do that, Anne," I said very gently, for I couldn't think it; and yet her despairing tone alarmed me more than if she had been angry or deeply disturbed.

And then the others joined us, and the conversation became general. But, seemingly by tacit consent, the subject of the crime or the coming of the new detective was not touched upon. Even Mrs. Stelton seemed to feel the restraint that was upon us all, and for once refrained from making her usual flippant and ill-timed observations. The party broke up early, and we all went to our rooms. The men did not congregate in the smoking-room as usual, but parted on the landing with brief good-nights.

I, for one, felt heavy of heart. Anne's definite speech had frightened me, and I wondered if in sending for Stone I had precipitated the very calamity I wished to avert. But it was too late now for regret. I had put the matter in other hands, and I must abide by the consequences. And yet, though I could still hope for Anne's innocence, though my heart still whispered, "Anybody but Anne!" I was far from having the same confidence that I had felt earlier in the day.

The next morning Fleming Stone came. The moment I saw him, I was glad I had summoned him. He looked so strong, so capable, and so resourceful, that I knew instinctively he would reach the truth. And, after all, it was the truth we wanted—or ought to want.

We congregated in the drawing-room to meet him, and his reception was more like that of an honored guest than an official detective. He greeted each one individually and with the utmost cordiality and kindness. But after a few polite commonplaces of conversation, he rose alertly and declared himself ready to begin the business in hand.

"I assume I have the freedom of the house," he said, turning to Anne, who responded merely by a bow.

She was frightened, I could see that, and yet there was nothing in Fleming Stone's manner to inspire alarm. Indeed, he looked at her with an intent admiration, as he had done on his former visit, and I realized that he would give her every possible benefit of doubt.

"I shall go to the study first," he said, "and I should like to be accompanied only by Mr. Sturgis and Mr. Markham. After my investigations there, I may want to ask some questions of the rest of you." I wanted to feel that Stone was taking me with him because I might be of some assistance, but this vain hope was quickly shattered.

"I want you with me, Mr. Sturgis," he said, as we entered the study and he closed the door, "first, because you are my employer; and also because you are the only one of this household who cannot possibly be implicated in this crime."

I suppose I looked my amazement, for he went on, "That does not mean that all the rest are implicated, but you are the only one who I know is not."

"How do you know that, Mr. Stone?"

"First, from the letter you wrote me, which leaves you free of suspicion, while it leaves every one else open to the possibility of it. Second, because you had no motive for the deed."

"But I—"

"You needn't finish; I know you are deeply attracted to Mrs. Van Wyck, but you would not murder her husband in order to win her, and then send for me to come out here to discover the criminal!"

"No, I wouldn't," I replied, almost smiling at the way he put it. "And now, Mr. Stone, if I can help you in any way, I shall be only too glad."

"I think I shall not require help, thank you; I ask only freedom from interruption, and, possibly, answers to occasional questions."

If the words were a trifle curt, the tone was not at all so, and I willingly sat down, content to watch the great man at his work. Mr. Markham, also, watched Stone intently, and even offered suggestions now and then. But these, Stone dismissed with a mere word or two,—often with only a wave of his hand.

As I had surmised he would do, he scrutinized every part of the room; at first with sweeping glances, and then focussing his attention on various details. I had told him in my letter of the security with which the room was locked and bolted on the inside, and he examined all the fastenings of doors and windows with utmost care and interest.

"I think I can safely say," he remarked, "that I have never seen a room apparently so absolutely impossible of ingress. And yet some one entered and left while it was thus bolted and barred."

"It was not a suicide, then?"

"Certainly not. It was a case of wilful murder."

"Committed by an intruder?"

"Yes; by an intruder of exceeding cleverness, of marvellously cool nerve, and—"

"And of great physical strength?" I prompted.

"Not necessarily," said Stone, looking sharply at me. "I don't deduce especial strength."

I felt ashamed, for I realized in a sudden flash that I had said that hoping to learn that his thoughts were not directed toward Anne.

"What—what did this intruder do with the weapon he used?" I stammered, partly to hide my confusion.

"He left it behind him, in plain view of every one. I fear, Mr. Sturgis, you are unobservant."

"Wait a moment," I cried, stung by his evident scorn of what we had done, or, rather, what we had failed to do. "Do you mean to tell me that the weapon is even now in this room?"

"It is; and in plain sight."

"Don't tell me where; let me find it for myself," I cried, gazing wildly around.

"Find it if you can, but as you have overlooked it all these days, how can you expect to see it now—?"

"I'm completely mystified," I said. "We searched this room so carefully for the pearls, that I would have sworn we must have found a weapon, had there been any to find. Show it to me, Mr. Stone."

"There it is;" and Fleming Stone pointed quietly to a bill-file which stood on the desk. It was of the ordinary type, with a heavy bronze standard and a long, sharp, upright spike. The bills and papers on it reached nearly to the top, but as soon as my attention was drawn to it, I realized that with the bills removed it would indeed be a deadly weapon, and would correspond in every way to the weapon which the doctor declared must have been used.

"I can only suppose," I said, "that it escaped our attention because of its very obviousness."

"Not only that," said Stone, "but it was inconspicuous, being nearly covered with the bills; and, moreover, you looked only for a definite weapon, and not for an ordinary implement used as one."

"How did you come to notice it so quickly?"

"Because you had told me no weapon could be found, with the exception of the possible stiletto. And that did not greatly impress me, for no one would leave evidence of a crime in so simple a hidingplace. Even now I believe that bill-file to be the criminal's weapon, only because I can discover no other. But let us look at it. If we find a particle of blood-stain on the papers, I think we may have no further doubt."

Fleming Stone carefully lifted the bills from the metal rod that pierced them. Drawing a lens from his pocket, he examined the bill-file and several of the papers. "It was used to kill Mr. Van Wyck," he declared. "It was carefully wiped off and the bills returned to it. The particles of blood remaining on it are scarcely perceptible to the naked eye, but may clearly be seen through the magnifying-glass. You may perceive, also, some faint stains around the holes in the papers where they slid down the spike. As this is vital evidence, I will put it safely away."

Fleming Stone put the file with its papers in a small cupboard of the desk, which he locked and then took out the key.

After that, for a long time, Markham and I sat silently watching him as he proceeded with his scrutiny of the room. Occasionally he examined something through his glass, occasionally he picked up a scrap of something from the floor and put it in his notebook or pocket. At last I could contain myself no longer, and I burst out with,

"Mr. Stone, do you know how the murderer got in and out?"

"I do not," he replied. "I haven't the faintest idea. But since a human being did do so, another human being may discover how."

I felt that he was avoiding the masculine pronoun on purpose, and again my heart sank, as I feared for Anne.

After an hour or so, though it seemed ages, Fleming Stone declared his investigation of the room completed, and announced his desire to see next some of the servants. I took him across the house to the kitchen quarters, and in the butler's pantry we found a footman and two maids.

After a quick glance at the faces of the trio, Mr. Stone interrogated the more intelligent-looking of the maids. "When express packages arrive," he said to her, in his pleasant way, "who attends to them?"

"A footman, sir," said the girl, with an air of proud importance at being questioned.

"What footman? This one?"

"Yes, sir. That's Jackson, sir. He 'most always takes the express parcels."

"Ah, then you can speak for yourself, Jackson. On the day of your master's death, did any express parcels arrive?"

"Yes, sir," replied Jackson. "I remember there were three came that morning."

"What was in them?"

"Supplies for the pantry, sir. Mostly bottles and jars, sir."

"And what were they packed in—excelsior?"

"Yes, sir; excelsior and straw."

"And was there no other parcel, containing china or glass?"

"There was another, sir, but not by express. Mr. Sturgis brought it. That was glass, and it was taken to Mrs. Van Wyck's room."

Fleming Stone turned to me. "What was the packing, Mr. Sturgis?" he said.

"I don't know," I replied, greatly mystified at this turn of affairs. "I brought a glass vase as a gift to Mrs. Van Wyck, but she opened the box when I was not present."

"I emptied the box, sir," volunteered Jackson, "and it was full of tissue paper cut into little scraps."

"Yes, of course," agreed Stone. "That is what a fine piece of glass would naturally be packed in. That is all. Thank you, Jackson."

Slowly and thoughtfully, Stone walked back through the house. He detained me a moment as we passed through the dining-room. "You want me to go on with the case, Mr. Sturgis," he said, "wherever the results may lead—?"

I shuddered at this question, coming right on top of his discovery of Anne's glass vase. I could see no possible connection between my innocent gift and the Van Wyck tragedy, but there must have been one in Stone's mind.

However, I replied " Yes," knowing that I must know the truth, whatever it might be.

CHAPTER 19: THE TWO CARSTAIRS

WE all three went back to the study. Stone looked thoughtful, even puzzled.

"It is the most mysterious case I have ever known," he said.

"I heard you say once," I observed, "that the deeper the apparent mystery, the easier the solution."

"And that is true, in a way, Mr. Sturgis. A simple commonplace case with little mystery and much seemingly direct evidence, is often more difficult than a case which presents startling and strange features."

"Well," put in Mr. Markham, "if another mystery will help you in the matter, here it is, "and he handed Fleming Stone the typewritten letter.

"A letter always means a great deal," said Stone, as he scrutinized the address.

Markham and I watched him almost breathlessly as he drew out the letter and read it.

He studied both the sheet and the envelope for a few moments, and then looked up and said quietly, "the letter is a decoy."

"We thought of that," said Mr. Markham, eager to seem astute; "and it was mailed the day of Mr. Van Wyck's death, and the letter was written on the typewriter in this very room!"

"Mailed in the morning and received in the afternoon," agreed Stone, glancing at the postmarks. "It was written on two different typewriters, and to my mind this clearly tells the whole story. I am willing to aver that whoever sent this missive abstracted from Mrs. Van Wyck's room, perhaps from her waste basket, a complete letter probably an unimportant one,—which she had

received duly in her Friday afternoon mail. That letter
bore writing only on its first page;—it might have been a
printed advertisement. Whoever was managing the affair,
tore off that first page and utilized this second half of the
sheet for this letter, bringing it in here to write. Then it
was an easy matter to put it back in the envelope, thus
making it seem like a letter which had come duly through
the mail. It was brought to you, a bit of faked evidence, —
and I doubt if Mrs. Van Wyck ever saw the letter at all."

"But it was found in a book she was reading the very
night the crime occurred," said Mr. Markham.

"You mean you have been told that it was. Have you
asked Mrs. Van Wyck, herself—?"

"Would she admit it, if she were guilty?" said
Markham with a triumphant air of having said
something clever.

"Not in so many words, perhaps; but surely one could
judge from her manner. Now then, to discover who did
write this letter; which ought not to be at all difficult. It
does not bear on its face evidence of being the work of
either of David Van Wyck's children."

"No," agreed Mr. Markham, eagerly, "they would
scarcely connive with their step-mother in such a deed."

"I don't mean that! There was no conniving. Nobody
really wrote to Mrs. Van Wyck that she should do this
thing, and he would protect her! The thing is a fraud, I
tell you, and was written merely to throw suspicion on
Mrs. Van Wyck." I could have hugged Stone for this.
Wherever his deductions might lead it would certainly be
toward anybody but Anne!

"Of course," he went on, "this in no sense exonerates
Mrs. Van Wyck; nor does it prove anything except that
some one chose this means of throwing suspicion on her.
It was cleverly done, and yet it is, after all, a clumsy piece
of work, for it bears on its face the stamp of fraud.
Anyone ought to know to-day, that the fact of using
different typewriters would give away the game.

Therefore, it was written by some one who—by the way, are there any French people in the house?"

Stone asked this question, after a further perusal of the letter.

"Yes," said Mr. Markham, quickly, "there are two of them."

"I have a strong conviction that one of them wrote this letter," said Stone.

"Carstairs! I told you so!" and Mr. Markham looked elated; "he's Mr. Van Wyck's valet, and I knew all along he was in connivance with Mrs. Van Wyck."

Fleming Stone looked at him, "I have told you," he said, "this letter does not mean connivance. Would this valet, for any reason, want to throw suspicion on Mrs. Van Wyck—?"

"I don't know," and Mr. Markham looked positively sullen because Fleming Stone's deductions did not seem to agree with his own.

"Who is the other French person—?" asked Stone.

"It's Carstairs' mother," I said. "She is housekeeper here."

"Carstairs is not a French name."

"No, Mr. Stone; but she is a Frenchwoman. I believe her husband was an Englishman, and her son seems to have the traits of both. Mr. Van Wyck considered him an exceptionally good valet."

"Please send for them both," was Fleming Stone's order, and Markham rang the bell. The two Carstairs came in together, and to my mind the mother looked like a lioness defending her young. Surely whatever traits this strange woman possessed, her maternal instinct was among the strongest. She looked defiant as she entered, and putting Carstairs in the background, she herself took a chair near Stone, and seemed ready to answer questions.

Of course, we had told Fleming Stone everything we knew concerning the whole matter. He knew of Carstairs' joy ride, and of his fright lest it be discovered. His gaze went past the mother and fastened on the white-faced young man.

"Carstairs," he said, in a quiet pleasant tone, "you really needn't feel so frightened. You didn't kill your master,—you had no hand in it. Now, secure in the knowledge of your innocence, why are you so filled with alarm?"

"I'm n-not, sir," and though the valet looked greatly relieved at Stone's words, he was still nervously agitated.

But the look of relief on Mrs. Carstairs' face was unmistakable. A light spread over her whole countenance, and she looked like one who had narrowly escaped disaster.

Fleming Stone looked at her intently. She returned his gaze without fear, even with a trace of her usual seductive manner; but he seemed to look straight through any mannerism to her very soul. After a moment, he said, and his words shot out suddenly:

"Mrs. Carstairs, had you any reason for wishing to fasten this crime on Mrs. Van Wyck, except to direct suspicion from your own son?"

The housekeeper's eyes blazed. "I hate her!" and the exclamation seemed wrung from her by Stone's compelling eyes.

"Why?" The inquiry v/as in the most casual tones.

"Because she—"

"Mother!" young Carstairs interrupted her; "what are you saying? Collect yourself! You make a mistake!"

Mrs. Carstairs gave one frightened, bewildered glance at her son, and then like a flash she changed the whole expression of her face.

"I beg your pardon," she said, gently; "I spoke without thinking. I really have no animosity toward Mrs. Van Wyck. I did feel a slight jealousy when she married a man who had promised to marry me. But that is past now, and I bear her no ill will."

"You are telling deliberate untruths," said Stone, straightforwardly; "but it does not matter; I have learned what I have wanted to know. Now Mrs. Carstairs you have no notion who sent this letter to Mrs. Van Wyck, I suppose—?"

"Certainly not," she returned, disdainfully eying the letter Stone held up.

"You found it in a book, as you described to Mr. Markham?"

"Yes."

"And you came and asked Mr. Sturgis for it, saying that he might keep a copy of it?"

"I did."

"I have concluded, Mrs. Carstairs, to grant that request, if you will make the copy yourself."

"I cannot use a typewriter, Mr. Stone. I'm not familiar with the work."

The valet gave an involuntary glance of surprise at his mother, but immediately dropped his eyes again.

She can use a typewriter! I thought to myself, and won't admit it!

But Stone said, lightly, "Oh, that doesn't matter. Just write with a lead pencil. Here is one."

"I prefer not to do it," and Mrs. Carstairs looked at the great detective with the air of a frightened animal, who does not understand into what snare it is being led.

"Why not?" asked Stone.

"Because—because—"

"You seem to have no reason for refusing. It is a small matter. Kindly make a copy at my dictation."

He offered a pencil and a paper pad to Mrs. Carstairs, and though she hesitated, she finally took them, as there seemed to be nothing else to do. In a low, clear tone, Fleming Stone read the sentences from the letter, waiting after each until Mrs. Carstairs had written it.

The woman looked utterly miserable. It was evident that she could not see why she had to do this, but she feared some underlying reason that boded ill for her.

Inexorably, Stone continued. One after another, the short, direful sentences fell from his lips. Mrs. Carstairs grew whiter and her fingers almost refused to hold the pencil, but with indomitable courage she persevered to the end.

After the last word, Stone held out his hand for the paper, and she mutely handed it to him. The rest of us sat spellbound. There was nothing theatrical in the episode, it was the quietest possible procedure, and yet the incident seemed fraught with intense mystery and importance.

Fleming Stone gave the merest glance at the paper, tore it into tiny bits and threw it into the waste-basket.

"Mrs. Carstairs," he said, and his tone was almost careless; "you wrote that letter yourself on the typewriter in this room. It was cleverly done. You used the blank half of a letter Mrs. Van Wyck had already received and the envelope it came in. You pretended that she had received and read this letter. Now will you tell us just why you did this, or would you prefer to explain it to the coroner later?"

"I didn't "

"It is useless to, say you didn't," interrupted Stone. "The proof is positive. Now I'll repeat my question of some time ago. Did you wish to incriminate Mrs. Van Wyck merely to divert suspicion from your son, or for any other reason?"

Again anger and rage gleamed from Mrs. Carstairs' eyes. She was about to, burst into a torrent of language, when she controlled herself, glanced at her son, and said in a low, even thrilling tone: "Only to save my son from possible suspicion!"

"Again, you're telling an untruth, madam," said Stone, as if it were a matter of no moment.

"You are rather expert at it. However, if you'll take my advice, you will do wisely to adhere to that statement! Let me suggest that you keep your other reason to yourself. You may go."

For the first time in my experience, I saw Mrs. Carstairs' face wear a beaten look. She rose from her chair, a vanquished woman. But she had nerve enough to make a slight mocking bow as, accompanied by her son, she left the room.

"The whole matter of that letter means nothing" said Fleming Stone; "the case is still the deepest mystery to me. I saw at once after I learned Mrs. Carstairs had written that letter, that her prime motive was to save that idolized son of hers from accusation or suspicion. But another reason, was her hatred of Mrs. Van Wyck. I advised her to keep that to herself, and as I imagine she will do so, I doubt if she can do any more harm."

"How are you sure she wrote the note?" asked Mr. Markham, and I, too, waited with eagerness for the answer.

"It was a random shot," said Stone, smiling a little; "although it was quite evident how the thing was done. But you remember, I asked you if there were any French people about. As you see, in this letter, the word committee is spelled with one " M." While that might be a mere verbal error, it gave me the impression that the note was written by a French native. For their word is 'comite,' and while the writer of the note is familiar with the English tongue, that is a tricky word for a Frenchman to spell, because of the double letters. However, that proof needed confirmation, so I simply asked the lady to write the note from my dictation; and, if you please, she misspelled 'committee' in exactly the same way! Even then, it might have been that the son wrote it,—or any one else, for that matter, but when I declared with conviction that she had written it, she was unable to deny it!"

"It all sounds so simple, now that you explain it," I said, with a feeling of chagrin that I had not noticed the misspelled word.

"That particular bit of a mystery was simple of solution," said Stone, but it helps us not a bit with the main issue.

At Stone's request, we went in search of Anne.

We found her in the music-room with Archer. They were in close conversation, and I had no doubt he was urging her again to give him the right to protect her. I knew Archer felt, as I did, that all usual conventions were to be ignored in such circumstances as these we were experiencing. Fleming Stone spoke directly to Anne, and his calm, pleasant manner seemed to imbue her with an equal quietness of demeanor. She even almost smiled when Stone said, "Please don't think me over-intrusive, Mrs. Van Wyck, but will you tell me what gown you wore at dinner last Friday evening?"

"Certainly," said Anne, rising. "If you will come to my room, I will show it to you."

Although uninvited, Archer and I followed. On reaching Anne's dressing-room, she took from a wardrobe the beautiful yellow satin gown, which I well remembered, and which now seemed to mock at the sombre black robe she wore.

Stone looked at the gown admiringly, and seemed to show a special interest in the frills and jabots of the bodice. Truly, this man's ways were past understanding! What clue could he expect to find in this way?

"And when you came to your room that night, did you keep on this gown until you prepared to retire?"

"No," said Anne, looking at him wonderingly; but even as she looked, her eyes fell before his and she continued in a hesitating way, "No, I changed into a negligee gown."

"May I see that—?" asked Stone pleasantly.

This time, it seemed to me, with reluctance, Anne took from the wardrobe a charming boudoir robe of chiffon and lace. It was decorated with innumerable frills and rosettes, and again Stone seemed eagerly interested in the trimmings. He even picked daintily at some of the bows and ruches, saying lightly, "I am not a connoisseur in ladies' apparel, but this seems to me an exquisite confection."

"It is," replied Anne. "It is Parisian." But she spoke with a preoccupied air, and I knew she was deeply anxious as to the meaning of all this. She hung the gown back in its place, and then Stone seated himself, after having courteously placed a chair for her.

"I warned you I should ask a few questions, Mrs. Van Wyck," he began; "so please tell me, first, how you occupied the time before you retired that evening?"

Anne's embarrassment had vanished, and she looked straight at her questioner as she replied in even tones, "I'm afraid I did nothing worth-while. I wrote one or two notes to friends, glanced through a book about Gardening, tried on a new hat, and then unpacked a glass vase which Mr. Sturgis brought me, because I prefered not to trust that task to a servant."

"And your maid was here when you finally retired—?"

"No, I had dismissed Jeannette earlier, and told her she need not return."

"And did you leave your rooms late that night?"

"No."

"Not at all?"

"No."

But Anne was fast losing control of herself. Her voice trembled, and her large eyes were fixed on Stone's face. His expression was one of infinite pity, and he said gently, "Please think carefully, and be sure of what you are saying."

"I am sure," murmured Anne, and then Archer leaned over and whispered to her. What he said I do not know, but it must have been an accusation of some sort, for Anne turned scarlet and stared at Archer with angry eyes. She glanced at her bookshelves, and then back at Archer and then at Stone, and finally, with a look of pathetic appeal, directly at me.

I knew she was asking my help, but what could I do? In a sudden desperate attempt to relieve her, for at least a moment, I turned the subject, and, touching the beautiful Florentine chest on the table beside me, I drew Stone's attention to it as a work of art.

"Yes," he agreed; "it is a fine piece. Worthy of holding the family heirlooms."

"Instead of which," I said lightly, "Mrs. Van Wyck uses it merely as a receptacle for old photographs." Anne's agitation seemed to be increasing, and, determined to keep Stone from addressing her for a few moments longer, I opened the chest to prove my words. Stone glanced carelessly at the old pictures, faded except round their edges, and then, suddenly rising, he picked up two or three and looked at them intently. A sudden light flashed into his eyes, and, turning to Anne, he said in tones of genuine admiration, "Wonderful, Mrs. Van Wyck! Positively splendid! I congratulate you."

I looked at him in amazement. There was no portrait of Anne among the old photographs he held, and what he meant I could not imagine.

But Anne knew. Sinking back in her chair, she covered her face with her hands and gave a low moan.

CHAPTER 20: THE MYSTERY SOLVED

JUST then Barbara and Morland came into the room. "What's the matter, Anne?" Morland asked. "Who's bothering you? I won't have it!"

He went to her and put his arm round her, and, seemingly encouraged by his strength and sympathy, Anne looked up and with an effort regained her poise.

"They're mine!" she exclaimed, addressing herself to Stone, while her dark eyes flashed defiance at him.

"I don't doubt it," he replied, and then he looked at her in a perplexed way. For a moment these two exchanged glances, and it seemed as if they had superhuman powers of reading each other's thoughts. Then Stone gave a little nod, straightened himself up, and said, "We must go on, whatever the outcome."

Then, speaking to us all, generally, he said, "I have found the missing pearls—I can lay my hand upon them at any moment. Before I do so, does the one who took them from the study wish to say so?"

Archer looked at Anne, but I looked at Morland. I had a feeling that Morland had taken those pearls; but, if so, he showed no evidence of guilt at this moment.

Fleming Stone looked at no one in particular, and after a moment's pause he said, "Then I will simply hand them to their owner."

He went to the book-shelves, and without hesitation took down a thick volume. It was an oldfashioned photograph album, fastened with two ornate gilt clasps. Slowly snapping these open, he opened the book. The photographs from several of the leaves had been removed, and in the cavity thus made, wrapped in blue cotton, was the Van Wyck pearl necklace!

Amid the exclamations of surprise, I was silent, for I realized instantly that those photographs in the gilt chest were the ones taken from the album to make room for the pearls; and that I—*I* had deliberately shown those photographs to Stone, and thereby offered his quick intellect a clue to the hiding-place!

"They are mine!" cried Anne. "It was no theft! My husband gave them to me, and I had a perfect right to take them when I chose, and hide them where I chose. But because I took them from the safe in the study, you need not think that I killed my husband! I took them—the day before!"

"Anne," exclaimed Archer in a warning voice, "tell the truth, dear—it will be better."

"But you did go into the study late that night, Mrs. Van Wyck," said Stone quietly.

"How do you know?" flashed Anne.

"For one thing, your maid saw you coming from the study shortly after midnight. But also, I found in there, on the fur rug in front of the safe, two small scraps of the shredded tissue-paper from the box which you unpacked. I found also two, bits in the rosettes of the negligee gown that you wore, and I'm sure that the bits on the rug fell from your gown as you took the pearls from the safe. I do not deny your right to take them; nor your right to hide them in the exceedingly clever place you selected. But I must ask you to admit if this is true."

"It is true," said Anne, as if at the end of her endurance, and then she fainted.

We went away from the room, leaving her with Barbara and the maid; and as none of us felt inclined to talk, we drifted apart.

Fleming Stone seemed more than ever thoughtful and preoccupied. I would have talked with him, but he asked to be left to himself, and went directly to the study.

Soon after this, luncheon was announced, and we gathered round the table in a desperate effort to throw off the gloomy fear that overhung us.

At first the conversation was on general subjects, Stone leading the way with his kindly and courteous remarks.

But all at once Anne lifted her great eyes, and, looking straight at Stone, said, "I know you think I killed my husband, Mr. Stone, but I did not. And why should I do so, to get those pearls, since they were my own, anyway?"

I thought perhaps Fleming Stone would answer this question directly, but instead he said, "Were you not anxious to prevent his gift to the library?"

Then Morland spoke in a terse, hard voice:

"You mean by that, Mr. Stone, that Anne took the Deed of Gift from my father's desk. That is not true, for I took it myself."

"You did?" said Stone, looking at him sharply.

"Yes, I did. I told the truth when I said I left the study before Lasseter did. But I don't think Lasseter knew this, and he thought I was there when he went away. But a little later I returned. My father was not there; the outside door was open, and I think he had stepped out on the terrace. However, I took the deed, and I have it in my possession still; but as it is unsigned, it is of no value to anybody. But I did not kill my father, and I'm telling about the deed to exonerate Anne from any suspicion of having taken it."

Anne cast a grateful look at Morland, and then continued to look at him, but with a changed expression. I could follow her thoughts, or at least I thought I could, and I thought she was wondering if, after all, Morland had killed his father. Perhaps they had quarrelled over the deed, and Morland was misrepresenting the scene.

At any rate, the net of suspicion was drawing close round the two, Morland and Anne. My heart sickened as I realized that it must have been one or the other of these, and that Fleming Stone's unerring skill would yet discover which.

"It is unnecessary to assert innocence until guilt is suspected," said Stone, in a calm voice; "and until we learn how a murderer could get in and out of that locked room, we can accuse no one; nor can we assert that it was not a case of suicide." And then he determinedly changed the subject; nor would he allow it to be brought up again during the meal. But as we left the table, Stone spoke low to me.

"Lead the whole crowd out on the terrace," he said, "and keep them there for an hour or so. On no account let them come into the house, or at least not into the study. I must be uninterrupted for an hour, at least, and then the mystery will be solved."

He had not set me a difficult task. For some reason, the members of the little group seemed quite willing to stay out of doors. We strolled down to a large arbor on the lawn, and sat there talking, sometimes all together, and sometimes in twos and threes. After a while Markham joined us, and inquired how far Mr. Stone had progressed in his investigations. Anne told him frankly enough that she herself had taken the pearls from the safe, and Morland repeated his admission of having taken the deed. Mr. Markham was excited over these revelations, but the strange apathy that had settled down on our people was not greatly stirred by his comments. Presently Archer and Beth Fordyce went off for a walk around the garden. Mrs. Stelton asked me to go, too, but I declined, as I had my work of keeping the people out of the house.

It was just about an hour before Stone rejoined us. He greeted Mr. Markham pleasantly enough, and then turned to me. "As my employer," he said, "shall I make my final report to you?"

"To all of us," I replied. "I asked you to come here, but Mrs. Van Wyck and David Van Wyck's children are quite as much entitled to hear your report as I."

"Let us all go to the study, then," said Stone. "Where is Mr. Archer?"

"He went down through the lower gardens with Miss Fordyce," I replied.

"Mr. Markham," said Stone, "suppose you go after them." He added a few words to Markham which I did not hear, and then we all went to the study.

"I can tell you all in a few words," said Mr. Stone. "We know that Mrs. Van Wyck took the pearls from the safe, and that Mr. Morland Van Wyck took the paper from his father's desk. But neither of these had any hand in Mr. Van Wyck's death. Mr. Van Wyck was murdered later that same night. He was stabbed with this bill-file;" and Stone produced the file in evidence. "After killing Mr. Van Wyck, the murderer himself carefully fastened all the doors and windows, and left the room by a secret exit. This is the explanation of the sealed room, and I will now show you where the secret passage is. I did not know myself until during the last hour. I came in here positive that there was some such way of egress, and after a careful search I found it. As you see, the study is joined to the main house only by one corner, which laps the corner of the house for a space of about ten feet. This ten feet on the ground floor gives space for the connecting doorway which is usually used. The study is the height of two full stories of the house, but the study has only one story, and therefore an unusually high ceiling. The deep cornice has an immense cartouche ornamenting each corner. It seemed to me that behind this cartouche in the corner that touches the house was the only possibility of a secret exit from this room."

All eyes turned at once to the great shield-shaped affair of which he spoke. It was quite large enough to conceal a secret door, but at a height of twentyfive feet or more from the floor, it was entirely inaccessible.

"It seems inaccessible," said Stone, following our thoughts, "and there is no ladder or possibility of one anywhere about. But I was so sure that my theory was the true one that I examined the floor in that corner and found several tiny flakes of plaster that had fallen. Then I was certain that the secret exit had been used recently. I went in the house, and upstairs to the room in which the secret passage —if there was one—must necessarily open. I found in the back part of a deep cupboard a panel, and by dint of search I found a spring which caused the panel to open. I then discovered that I was directly back of the great cartouche. In a word, the passage is an exit from this room. I will now show you the means of using it."

We watched with breathless attention while Fleming Stone mounted the spiral staircase and walked the length of the little gallery. At the end he stood with his hand on the end rail, quite four feet from the cartouche.

"Note the beautiful simplicity of it," he said. Merely loosening a bolt on the under side of the end railing caused the whole end of the balcony to fall outward. As it did so, the great end bracket beneath swung the other way, acting as a counterweight, and what had been the end railing of the gallery was now a horizontal bridge straight across to the cartouche. Moreover, mechanism in the wall had at the same time raised the outer shell of the cartouche, which was hinged at the top, and disclosed a small doorway.

"That is all," said Mr. Stone, speaking to us from the gallery. "As I said, it is beautifully simple. Once unbolted, a person's weight serves to throw down the railing as a bridge, and open the cartouche. Now you will see that, as I step off and through this doorway, the removal of my weight causes the railing to swing back to place, and the cartouche to close."

Stepping off the railing upon a ledge and through the door, Stone disappeared, and the mechanism worked exactly as he had said. A moment later he reappeared.

"You see," he resumed, "that is the way David Van Wyck's murderer left this room, after securely locking it with the intent to involve the affair in deepest mystery. You all know, I suppose, who occupies the room into which the secret passage opens on the second floor of the house."

"I know," said Anne. "It is Condron Archer."

"And Mr. Archer has gone away," said Fleming Stone significantly. "I have sent Mr. Markham after him, but, as I understand it, I was employed here to solve a mystery, and not to arrest a criminal. In fact, I have not proved that Mr. Archer is the criminal. But I think no one doubts it." It was at this point that Beth Fordyce returned to us. "Oh, Anne," she said, "Mr. Archer said that he had to go away very suddenly. He had had a telegram, or something, and he asked me to tell you good-by for him, and to give you this letter."

"It is his confession," said Anne, in a low voice, as she took the letter from Beth. "I felt sure of it all the time. Raymond, will you read it aloud?"

I was touched at the confidence she showed in me, and, taking the letter, I opened it. It bore no address, and began abruptly thus:

"This is not a confession, but an explanation of why I killed David Van Wyck. I know now that Fleming Stone's penetration will discover the secret passage, which Mr. Van Wyck himself explained to me a few days before his death. And so I am going away—not fleeing from justice, but because I do not look upon myself as a criminal. I killed Mr. Van Wyck, not in self-defense, but in defense of one far dearer to me than myself. Last Friday night, after having gone to my room at eleven o'clock, I came downstairs again about midnight, with no intent other than a stroll on the terrace. I had been there but a few moments when Mr. Van Wyck joined me. I do not wish to repeat his conversation, but I realized what a vicious, cruel, and even diabolical husband he was to the woman I adored. I speak frankly of this adoration, for it is no secret. David Van Wyck talked of his wife in a way that made my blood boil, and I was about to tell him so when, his attention attracted by a sound in the study, he beckoned to me, and we looked in at the window. Mrs. Van Wyck was taking the pearls from the safe. As we watched, she carried them from the room, closing the door behind her. David Van Wyck drew me into the study with him, and exclaimed in fiendish glee, 'Now I have her where I want her! I shall denounce her as a thief, and see if she will then be so high and mighty toward me!' I begged him not to do this, whereupon he accused me of being in love with his wife, and made other wicked assertions that I could not stand. He repeated his intention to give away all his money, to get back the pearls, and to denounce Anne as a thief; and he became, I really think, momentarily insane in his rage. Possibly I too lost my mind, but I snatched up the bill-file, tore off the papers, and stabbed him in a moment of white-hot anger. I carefully locked up the study, hoping the deed might thus be an insoluble mystery. I left the room by the secret exit, which leads directly to the cupboard in the bathroom adjoining my bedroom. It was through this panel I had disappeared the night Sturgis looked for me. I went back to the study to see if I had left behind me any incriminating evidence. I found none, but after Mr. Stone deduced Mrs. Van Wyck's presence in the study, by scraps of tissue paper, I have no doubt he will in some way trace mine.

"As to my act,—I will not call it a crime,—I do not regret it. I have saved Mrs. Van Wyck from the cruelties of a monster, and I am glad of it. But I refuse to .pay the penalty for this, and so I shall disappear forever from the country. I could not do this if I thought I could ever win my heart's desire. But I know, Anne, that in the after years you will find joy and peace with a man who is worthy of your regard, though it pierces my heart to admit it. But even if through crime, Anne, I have saved you from the further despotism and insults of a brute; and the knowledge of that is my reward. "

CONDRON ARCHER."

I finished reading, and there was a death-like silence. I think not one in the room wished to prosecute Archer; I think each heart was praying that Markham might not find him.

"I told Mr. Markham to detain Mr. Archer if he found him," said Fleming Stone slowly. "I fear that I regret doing so."

"He won't find him," said Anne, and as if in proof of her words, Mr. Markham came in.

"Mr. Archer has disappeared," he said. "I thought he might go by train, and I waited at the station, but he didn't. Do you want him very much?"

"No," said Anne. "We don't want him at all. Don't look for him any more, Mr. Markham." And then, as the tears flooded her eyes, she turned to me, and, putting her trembling hand through my arm, she let me lead her out into the sunlight. There was no more mystery. The secret of the cartouche explained all.

The two Carstairs were dismissed from the Van Wyck service without punishment. For Anne never knew of the villainous note that had been written to bring trouble to her.

We never saw Archer again; and between Anne and myself his name has never been spoken. Buttonwood Terrace was sold, and the family separated. Morland went to the city to live, and Barbara went for a trip abroad, with Mrs. Stelton. But they may wander where they will,—it matters not to me; for after a time, Anne is going to crown my life with happiness, and I well know I shall never want anybody but Anne.

THE END

Other Resurrected Press Mysteries From Carolyn Wells

A Chain of Evidence
Anybody But Anne
In The Onyx Lobby
Raspberry Jam
Spooky Hollow
The Clue
The Curved Blades
The Diamond Pin
The Gold Bag
The Man Who Fell Through the Earth
The Mystery Girl
The Mystery of the Sycamore
The Room With The Tassels
The Vanishing of Betty Varian
The White Alley
Vicky Van

Resurrected Press Mysteries From Louis Tracy

The Albert Gate Mystery
Four men murdered and a fortune in diamonds belonging to the Turkish Sultan stolen, while the Foreign Office official in charge has gone missing. Was it a common jewelry theft or was it a case of international intrigue? This is the question that barrister detective Reginald Brett must solve.

The Bartlett Mystery
When Ronald Tower is murdered on his way to a bridge game on the yacht Sans Souci it at first appears a common crime. But as Rex Carshaw finds, a tragic case of mistaken identity leads to political scandal among the rich and powerful of New York.

The Strange Case of Mortimer Fenley
When the wealthy Mortimer Fenley is struck down by a shot from an express rifle on the steps of his mansion, detectives Winter and Furneaux of Scotland Yard must find the culprit. Was it the artist who claimed he was painting a picture at the time of the shot? The disaffected younger son? Or is there another suspect?

The Stowmarket Mystery
For five generations the Fergus-Hume family has been cursed. Each of the baronets has met a violent end. When the fifth baronet is found slain by a ceremonial Japanese dagger, suspicion falls on his cousin David. It falls to barrister detective Reginald Brett to prove his innocence and find the real murder in a case that spans two continents and as many centuries.

Resurrected Press Mysteries by J. S. Fletcher

The Orange-Yellow Diamond
When an elderly pawnbroker is murdered in the London parish of Paddington, a young, down on his luck writer is accused of the crime. But then it's found the pawnbroker had had in his possession an extraordinary South African diamond worth over eighty-thousand pounds —a diamond that's now missing. It falls to Melky Rubenstein to unravel the mystery and prove the young man's innocence.

The Middle Temple Murder
When an elderly man's body is found on the steps of chambers in the Midde Temple, one of the Inns of Court, it falls to newspaperman Frank Spargo and Detective-Sergeant Rathbury to solve the crime. The murdered man, for indeed it was murder, was found with no money or identification on his person except for a piece of paper with the name and address of a young barrister. Who is the victim? Why was he killed? Who is the murderer?

Scarhaven Keep
Bassett Oliver, the famed actor, has gone missing. When Oliver fails to show for a rehearsal, aspiring playwright Richard Copplestone finds himself sent to the small village of Scarhaven on the northern coast of England to track down the actors movements. What he finds is mystery. Find the answers as Copplestone unravels the mystery of Scarhaven Keep.

Resurrected Press Mysteries by Fergus Hume

The Green Mummy

Professor Braddock hoped to compare the burial practices of the Egyptians with those of the ancient Peruvians with his latest acquisition, the mummy of the last Inca, Caxas. But on arrival, the packing case proved to hold not the mummy, but the body of his assistant Sidney Bolton. It falls to Archie Hope to discover the murderer if he is to marry the professors step-daughter, Lucy Kendal. Who killed Bolton and where is the mummy? Was it the sea captain Hervey? The mysterious Don Pedro? Cockatoo the Polynesian servant? The professor, himself? And what has become of the emeralds? These are the questions that Hope must answer amongst the secrets of the past in The Green Mummy.

The Mystery of a Hansom Cab

"Truth is said to be stranger than fiction, and certainly the extraordinary murder which took place in Melbourne Friday morning goes a long way towards verifying that saying." Thus opens The Mystery of a Hansom Cab, the best selling mystery of the nineteenth century. When a man is found dead in a hansom cab one of Melbourne's leading citizens is accused of the murder. He pleads his innocence, yet refuses to give an alibi. It falls to a determined lawyer and an intrepid detective to find the truth, revealing long kept secrets along the way. Fergus Hume's first and perhaps most famous mystery... The Mystery Of A Hansom Cab.

Visit www.resurrectedpress.com

Resurrected Press Mysteries from the Dr. John Thorndyke Series

Dr. John Thorndyke Lecturer on Medical Jurisprudence and Forensic Medicine. Before Bones, before CSI, before Quincy, M.E– there was Dr. John Thorndyke solving the most baffling cases of Edwardian London using the latest tools of medical science. Read about his cases in:

The Eye of Osiris
John Bellingham, noted Egyptologist has vanished not once but twice in the same day. Now Dr, Thorndyke must unravel the tangled claims on his estate, solve the riddle of the missing man and find the "Eye of Osiris".

The Mystery of 31 New Inn
When Dr. Jervis is whisked away in a coach with no windows to an unknown location to treat a man in a coma from undivulged causes it is Dr. Thorndyke who must come up with the solution.

The Red Thumb Mark
The first of Dr. Thorndyke's cases finds him trying to prove the innocence of a young man accused of being a diamond thief despite the fact that his finger print was found at the scene of the crime.

John Thorndyke's Cases
More cases of medical mysteries as told by his trusted assistant Jervis, M.D. Eight stories of crime and deduction in Edwardian London.

Visit www.resurrectedpress.com

Resurrected Press Mysteries by John R. Watson & Arthur J. Rees

The Hampstead Mystery

High Court Justice Sir Horace Fewbanks found shot dead in his Hampstead home, a butler with a criminal past, a scorned lover and a hint of scandal. These are the elements of the Hampstead Mystery that Detective Inspector Chippenfield of Scotland Yard must unravel with the assistance of the ambitious Detective Rolfe. But will he be able to sort out the tangled threads of this case and arrest the culprit before he is upstaged by the celebrated gentleman detective Crewe. Follow the details of this amazing case at it plays out across Hampstead, London and Scotland until it reaches a stunning conclusion in the courts of the Old Bailey.

The Mystery of the Downs

When Harry Marsland was caught in a sudden down pour he sought shelter at Cliff Farm. Met at the door by a young woman clearly expecting someone else he is only too glad to get inside to wait out the storm. When they hear a noise upstairs in the deserted house they investigate only to discover the body of the farm's owner, Frank Lumsden, dead of a gunshot wound. Who then, killed Lumsden, and why? Who was the woman expecting and did she have any roll in the murder? These are the questions that private detective Crewe must answer in The Mystery of the Downs.

Visit www.resurrectedpress.com

Other Resurrected Press Mysteries

Mysteries on a Train

Before the Orient Express there was:

The Rome Express by Arthur Griffiths
A man is found dead in his first class sleeping compartment on the express from Rome to Paris. Who was his murderer? The Countess? The English General? His brother the clergy man? The maid who has disappeared? Is the French justice system up to solving the crime? Read about it in The Rome Express.

The Passenger from Calais by Arthur Griffiths
Colonel Basil Annesley finds he is the only passenger on the train from Calais to Lucerne. That is until a mysterious woman shows up at the last minute to book a compartment. Who is after her? What is her secret? Is she a criminal or a victim? Read about it in The Passenger from Calais

Visit us at www.resurrectedpress.com

About Resurrected Press

A division of Intrepid Ink, LLC, Resurrected Press is dedicated to bringing high quality, vintage books back into publication. See our entire catalogue and find out more at www.ResurrectedPress.com.

About Intrepid Ink, LLC

Intrepid Ink, LLC provides full publishing services to authors of fiction and non-fiction books, eBooks and websites. From editing to formatting, from publishing to marketing, Intrepid Ink gets your creative works into the hands of the people who want to read them. Find out more at www.IntrepidInk.com.